Divided By Design

By

Rodney D. Lewis

Published by Broadkast
The Media Factory
Copyright © 2020 Rodney D. Lewis
All Rights Reserved
Cover Design by Rommel Cumberbatch
Edited by Karieta Malone

Broadkast
The Media Factory
www.broadkastonline.com

For information about special discounts for bulk purchases by corporations, associations, and others, also contact the publisher, Broadkast The Media Factory.

This is a work of fiction. Names, characters, places and incidents are either the product of the author's imagination or are used fictitiously, and any resemblance to actual persons, living or dead, events, or locales is entirely coincidental.

ISBN Paperback: 978-1-64667-008-6
Printed in the USA

Dedication

This book is dedicated to my grandmother Eudene Yarde, affectionately called "Mommy." She was a woman like no other—hardworking, dedicated to family, loving, and giving. I have personally witnessed modern day miracles through observing her life and how even in her lack she had abundance to give to those in need.

I am eternally grateful to my three children for being daily beacons of inspiration. I am thankful to Kareesa and Janson for their undeniable support through this process.

CONTENTS

Introduction

Have you ever noticed that sometimes the things closest to you are the things you know the least about? This happens because with familiarity we become complacent. We think we know, so why probe? Our bodies, for example—we live with them but we never know their intricate workings. Similarly, as a black race, we find comfort in limited knowledge of ourselves, believing that we know ourselves since our very essence is wrapped in a blanket saturated with melanin. We tend, therefore, to ignore and reject new information concerning our blackness and become agitated, thinking we have heard it all before.

As a black man, I never paid any real attention to black history, black dynasties, black inventors, or anything black until recently, in my forties. I thought that I knew enough since I was raised as a black male, in a black community and everything around me was black. I knew our forefathers came to Barbados on a slave ship. What more was there to know? Black history was taught in schools. However, most academics seemed preoccupied with having intellectual discourse which mere mortals could not comprehend. Through my own personal observations and experiences, I attempted to convey the message of the black man's journey differently. I therefore implore all readers, regardless of race, to read the book from cover to cover with a clear mind, observing that there are fundamental areas addressed as the book evolves.

The book begins by introducing a nuclear family in Africa living harmoniously with man and nature when their lives were abruptly disrupted by power-hungry Europeans looking for cheap labour. Different aspects of the main characters' experiences were highlighted: how they were uprooted, transplanted, and then discarded. The book also opens a Pandora's Box of questions such as:

Was the black man already divided as a people, making it easier for the white man to remove them from their homeland and benefit by enslaving them for generations?

Could portraying the Messiah as a white man be one of the underlying reasons why blacks naturally adopt a position of servitude?

In the final chapter, the reader is engaged at a more esoteric level by the use of symbolism. If successful, the reader will have done introspection to form their interpretation of the imagery presented.

May you be enlightened...

The ramblings of a drunk, old white man...

"As a white man, whether I am overweight or slim, old or young, smart or illiterate, weak or strong, I am white! However, you are black, and that is what is wrong! If I were slim, I could choose to gain weight. If I were weak, I could become physically strong. If I were illiterate, I could learn to read.

"For you, however, it isn't that simple! You can't easily change your broad nose, your thick lips, your woolly hair or your black skin. Even if it were surgically possible, the essence of your blackness isn't superficial. It lives deep within.

"We all know why blacks were enslaved, but how was this accomplished by a few white men in a ship who sailed the seas with a handful of beads? Was it their masterful tongues spewing deceit and trickery that sowed the seed which filled the African slave traders' eyes with greed? What was it that caused black men to capture and chain their own, numerous black bodies, minds and souls?

"My forefathers were able to enslave your forefathers by paying them trinkets worth mud for human beings worth more than gold. Have you thought about who cleaned the ships? Who removed the sewage and scrubbed the floors making them spotless, without a trace of the preceded carnage, to prepare them for the next voyage?

However, to this day blacks still seem beholden to the bead giver, betraying, robbing, and killing each other for a morsel. They are still bleaching their very coats and weakening their manes to look like the white man, as though their blackness has no value."

Start processing...

PART ONE

CHAPTER ONE

Disruption

Amare was a tall, athletic, twenty-four-year-old man, who lived somewhere in a deep, untouched jungle on the continent of Africa. He had strikingly good looks, with eyes like pure fire which pierced the soul.

He was purposeful, strong-willed, helpful, competitive, and well- loved by everyone in his tribe. His tribe was a peaceful one, where everyone respected each other and worked together as a family.

Amare's wife Binta, whom he knew from childhood, was his number one fan. The twenty-one-year-old beauty, with her glowing ebony skin and long, strong locks which draped the contours of her perfectly sculpted features, was five months pregnant.

Amare and Binta already had a six-year-old son called Zarik. A bundle of joy, he was bright but mischievous like any other boy his age. Zarik idolized his father and followed him around as much as he could, paying avid attention to everything his father taught him.

Binta was an excellent cook and loved to experiment with different herbs and spices. This was one of the many ways she chose to show her husband how much she loved him. One morning, she awoke with an insatiable craving for a new recipe she had created with roasted fish, freshly picked green vegetables, and seasoned yams; so she bade her husband to go by the river to catch her favourite fish.

As the weather was bright and windy, she asked Amare to take Zarik, so that she could concentrate on preparing the dish. Amare got Zarik ready, grabbed his spear and his net, and they started the three-mile trek to the river.

As they made their way through the dense jungle, with its kaleidoscope of colours and immeasurable beauty, Amare was keen to teach Zarik the names of the myriad plants and fruits. The loud sounds of the birds and monkeys were like an unrehearsed choir but still pleasing to the ear.

At times, Zarik would run ahead with reckless abandon, falling and bruising his skin, while staying clear of the plants his father told him to avoid and having his fill of all the fruits he could reach. They knew they were close to the river as the scent of the air changed and they could hear the tranquil sounds of the water lapping the bank.

Zarik was so excited when he finally saw the water, as he was hot and sticky from perspiration and from the remnants of fruits on his face and fingers. As they carefully made their way down a slight embankment, they heard a loud explosion which caused the birds to scatter and the monkeys to erupt into a state of pandemonium.

Zarik, startled by the noise, fell awkwardly, bruising his knee on a rock. As Amare rushed to help him, four men appeared suddenly from a short distance away. Their skins were curiously strange and their faces had unfamiliar features. They were laughing and babbling in a strange tongue.

Amare held Zarik behind him and readied his spear as though hunting for wild boar. His blood raced through his veins, making his skin hot to the touch. He knew that he had to be brave for both himself and Zarik, who was so afraid that his fingernails were digging into his father's thigh.

The warrior in Amare wanted to fight; however, clearly outnumbered and with Zarik to protect, he decided against all odds to lift his son and run towards the village to warn the others. Sweat was pouring down Amare's face and burning his eyes. Zarik's loud breathing and crying were all that Amare could hear until another loud explosion rang through the air. He knew they were close and for the very first time in the forest, he felt like the prey being watched and tracked.

Amare knew he couldn't escape while carrying Zarik but protecting his son was his aim. He also did not want to lead the men back to his village and his wife Binta. He stroked Zarik's temple to calm him and placed his hand over his mouth for him to be silent. This was a nightmare for both father and son since neither of them in their wildest dreams could have imagined this would have happened to them. Amare rubbed mud on Zarik's face and body and covered him with grass, then hid him between shrubs to camouflage him. Shivering with fear, but knowing he had to be brave, Zarik lay as quietly as possible, barely blinking so as not to be caught unaware.

After he was satisfied that Zarik was safe, Amare kissed his son's exposed nose and whispered that he loved him. Amare cried as he left Zarik and cautiously headed deeper into the woods. The rain started to pour and drench the earth. Amare held his head back and opened his mouth to capture a few drops on his tongue. The sound of the wind as it howled was very familiar to Amare, but it felt eerie today as the trees made menacing gestures. Amare could hear the faint murmurings in the distance. Knowing the forest like the back of his hands, he crouched and moved stealthily, careful not to make a sound.

As he lay there, one of the strange fellows nearby saw him and pointed his raised stick in Amare's direction. This time, Amare noticed that fire and smoke came from it, along with a strange scent. The explosion was like before but ten times louder, ripping a piece of bark from a tree directly next to Amare's head.

Fragments from the tree covered Amare's hair and face; splinters and dust filled his eyes, which obscured his vision as he ran. However, he was quickly surrounded. With the precision of a true hunter, Amare threw his spear with all of his might, striking one of the strange fellows in the chest, whilst lunging at another with his bare hands, breaking his jaw with a single blow from his clenched fist. He would have easily ripped him to shreds but was prevented as he was placed in a chokehold by a black warrior from another tribe and struck in his face with the larger end of the stick.

As he fell to the ground, warm blood raced down his face and filled his eyes. The strange men kicked and spat on him before hog-tying him as he lay lifeless in the mud face down. "We have another big, black one here! Bloody bastard is strong and tough—we should get quite a penny for this ox," said one of the strange fellows.

Meanwhile, back where Zarik was hidden, he stayed silently for hours. The heavy rain had become a light drizzle and Zarik was thoroughly soaked. As he lay in the shrubs, tears formed in his eyes as he realized how long it had been silent. His father was always by his side, even when there was no danger, so it troubled him that he was not there now.

Needing to urinate, Zarik relieved himself, as he had done four times before, while remaining in the same position. Just as quickly as the comforting warmth of his urine flowed down his leg, distracting him from the cold of the night, something made its way up his inner thigh towards his testicles with purpose. On his thigh was the biggest, blackest centipede he had ever seen. His screams could be heard for miles as he abandoned his cover and scrambled to escape. Thinking himself to be free, he ran all the way home so as to avoid being recaptured by the three-hundred-legged creature.

When Zarik reached home he shouted frantically for his mother Binta while panting heavily. As he bent over to catch his breath, Zarik fainted when he saw that he had run all the way home with the centipede, which still clung to him and was now fully outstretched, reaching from his waist to just past his navel.

Back on the ship, Amare's violent, incessant screams enraged his captors, who would whip and beat him repeatedly, as though trying to break his will. The more they beat him and tore his flesh, the more noise he made.

Amare wanted to die, so he chose not to eat, but his captors were determined to keep him alive. With one sharp blow to his mouth they broke out his front teeth with a hammer, ripping them away from his gums. The pain was excruciating and as Amare screamed at the top of his lungs in agony, they silenced him by ramming a funnel through the space they had created in his mouth and force-fed him cornmeal pap not even fit for a pig, as his mouth filled with blood, causing him to gag and choke.

Amare had to endure being on this floating nightmare designed to transport human cargo in the most inhumane way possible. It was dark, dank, hot, and crammed with men, women, and children being treated like pigs headed to slaughter but with less wiggle room. The nostril-deep combination of decaying flesh, vomit, blood, and human waste created a suffocating blanket of sickness and suffering which dared Amare to inhale.

As the days turned into weeks and weeks into months, the conditions worsened as Amare and his fellowmen were forced to live in ankle-deep filth. Several men died from infections and their bodies were left to be devoured by maggots for days, until they were finally discarded like trash and thrown overboard.

The darkness was the darkest ever, with a hundred pairs of bewildered eyes fading daily as they cursed the very spirit that kept them alive. If ever there was a hell, this was it: the wailing, the cries, the cursing and men beating their heads against the wood trying to make the madness stop. One night as Amare wrestled with sleep, he momentarily lost the battle as his frail, weakened body keeled over, causing his head to rest on another captor's shit-filled butt crack. As this wasn't the most comfortable resting place, Amare kept shifting and contorting his body. His joints hurt and his skin was sore from sitting on the wood for so long. As he sat up, Amare wondered if Zarik had made it home safely to warn the others. He thought about Binta, wondering if she had given birth already.

Finally, the rocking stopped and for the very first time in three months, Amare saw the sun. Only a mere shadow of the man he was before, he was malnourished, frail, and barely able to stand on his own. His body was covered with sores and pus. He was paranoid and broken in spirit. His breath was horrid, and he smelt like hell. Excrement marinated his pores and his hair was drenched with urine. He had a very high fever and was coughing up blood and phlegm.

CHAPTER TWO

Transplanting

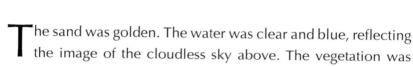

The sand was golden. The water was clear and blue, reflecting the image of the cloudless sky above. The vegetation was green and lush. The weather reminded him of home, which he was now thousands of miles away from, on an island he would later come to know as Barbados.

In that moment of nostalgic bliss, his thoughts about Binta and Zarik were abruptly interrupted by the cracking sound of a whip as it tore another piece of his weakened, bloody flesh. Still chained and shackled, Amare and approximately forty others were forced by horsemen to walk for miles in the hot sun, being tortured and beaten all the way to their destination. As he walked, he saw large open fields in the distance with silhouettes of several persons, black in complexion like himself, working while being watched by other horsemen with sticks.

The group came to a stop, where they were poked and inspected like cattle. Amare and five others were bought by a very wealthy plantation owner called Lynch. They were then separated from the others and led away.

Lynch was well into his forties and owned several acres of land. He was known to bid the highest amount for the strongest slaves. He took Amare and the others back to his plantation, where he made them strip naked, removing their loincloths, which were saturated with excrement and had become like a third layer of skin. As filthy as it was, the removal of this cloth was so symbolic to Amare, because for three long, arduous months it was all he had, besides his memories, that connected him to Binta and Zarik.

Buckets of water were then thrown on Amare to quell the stench and wash away the dirt. As he watched the dirt gradually loosen its grip, revealing his majestic blackness, his skin seemed to glisten as its high saturation of melanin embraced the sun's rays. Amare knew then that they could kill his body but not his spirit. No sooner had this thought crossed his mind than he was knocked to the ground, feeling a sharp pain in his ribs.

Clothes soiled with blood were thrown at him and he was ordered to put them on. "I paid quite a penny for you and as the sun is still high in the sky, I am going to work your ass till you die!" bellowed Lynch.

Amare was led to a field where he painstakingly toiled, ploughing the ground in silence until the sun fell from the sky and was replaced by the moon. He was then led to a small, dark wooden hut with a dirt floor, where he was given a tasteless mixture of corn and flour with a nasty utensil. His gum was still infected and sore from his teeth being knocked out on the ship.

As the hours passed, the night was silent and very humid. Amare was hot and miserable and as he lay on a piece of termite-infested plank, he saw the biggest rats ever! They were totally unmoved by his presence as they sniffed him curiously and ate the food he had left. As soon as he had drifted off to sleep, he

14

was awakened by loud shouting and was dragged from the hut to be hustled off to the field again.

It was early morning and it was still dark, as the sun was also awakening from its slumber. Regardless of what time he started working, he would still end when the sun retired for the evening. It didn't matter if Amare finished what he was ordered to do, there was always more work waiting for him. Oh, how he worked day after day, in the hot boiling sun, as he was whipped and cursed whenever he took a break. Once there was work to be done it didn't matter what day it was or what the conditions were, as there was never any ease from the blows and hard work. Amare was determined to kill these strange bastards who kept bruising his flesh.

That night back in his hut, Amare pondered how, when, and where he would convert his master into a lifeless lump of shit and bones. He realized that the more he conformed, the more perks he would receive so he played along, with his goal fixed. He also knew that he would need strength in numbers and strength in his body for this to be accomplished. So for the very first time in days, despite the pain he was experiencing from his infected gums, Amare ate all the food he was given.

The rats came as accustomed but were visibly confused when they were confronted with an empty bowl. Their squeaks were louder than before, as though they were arguing amongst themselves about the oddity that had occurred. Over time, as Amare got bigger and stronger the visits from the rats became less frequent, until they stopped altogether.

Amare was deliberately isolated from the other slaves, as his will didn't seem broken enough. He was forbidden to communicate with his tribesmen in their native tongue and was taught to speak the new language. This made plotting against these demons very challenging. He knew for his plan to be successful, they would have to find a way to speak in code. Amare watched and listened intently and gradually started to learn new words. Over time he found out that what he was calling a stick was actually a gun.

One Saturday morning, Amare observed a pig being slaughtered by a lighter-skinned slave with a very sharp knife. This slave was a very skilful butcher who took pride in his ability to expertly remove the lean meat from the animal's carcass for massa. This butcher was sure to only leave the entrails and extremities, which the flies covered and even the dogs rejected. However, the slaves fought for these scraps as it was their only source of meat.

On Sundays, the slaves wore the best of their soiled, stained garments, which only provided a superficial cover for the wounds hidden beneath, and gathered for church. The slaves who were beaten and tortured only moments ago were to rely on the teachings of the holy word which taught them to forgive and forget. The message of uncompromising obedience for massa was repeated like a mantra.

Massa contorted the message of the holy word to keep the slaves in bondage. Allegedly, in the book of Genesis and evidenced by their blackened skin, the slaves were cursed, through the "Curse of Ham." This must be true as massa said it was written in the word of God.

God in man—to be more specific, God in a white man—was called Jesus. In the story of Jesus, Jesus was the one punished. He was the one whose pretty white flesh was torn. He was the one made to carry the burden of mankind on his shoulders. He was the one whose blood was spilt as he was nailed to the cross. How come white massa never bore any pain?

This all-loving God, all-knowing God, all-merciful God, who sacrificed himself for all of mankind, seemed to have favourites, at least here on earth, where blacks were implored to endure suffering during their lifetime, in expectation of a reward after death. This teaching silenced and tied the hands of several slaves. It extinguished their passion and prevented them from fighting for their survival.

The pretence of love for fellowmen overshadowed the venomous hatred which existed between massa and the slaves. This pretence provided a temporary escape from reality until the service was over and the shepherds transformed into white wolves again, devouring the black sheep who followed them.

The days seemed longer than ever. Eventually, fifteen years passed since Amare was first captured. He continued working, learning, and planning. A lot of his friends died of exhaustion or were killed for insubordination throughout the years but one thing that remained constant was the steady replacement of slaves every three to four months. New bewildered souls, who would have travelled through hell and back, longing to die, were instead kept alive in a state of perpetual death. Amare's heart became heavy every time he looked these new victims in their eyes, knowing the journey they had travelled, leaving family and loved ones behind.

Lynch was aging but was still as ruthless as on day one. He acquired more land and needed more slaves than before to work on his plantation. The living conditions had become even more cramped, as several slaves were forced to sleep in the same small hut.

One evening, as Amare entered his hut a young man, still bound at the feet by rusty, tetanus-laden shackles, was lying in a foetal position holding his side as blood slowly eased its way between his fingers. He had been shot and was lucky to be alive; the pellet had only bruised his skin. His breathing was very faint and his temperature was extremely high, causing him to sweat profusely.

Amare could not see the youngster's face, as it was dark and stained with all manner of filth, but he did all he could to help him recover. Amare placed a cloth which he dampened by using his last cup of water on the young man's head until his temperature went down. Amare only drifted off to sleep when he was certain that the youngster would be ok.

Hours later, Amare opened his eyes in sync with the first light as it entered the hut, slowly peeling back the darkness, revealing the contours of the youngster's face. Suddenly, the youngster inhaled and frantically sprang to his feet as though he had been dreaming.

As Amare motioned to calm him, the youngster opened his eyes, rendering Amare speechless. "Zarik?! Oh my God, Zarik! My son!" he exclaimed in his native tongue. He was sure it was his son, as he had never forgotten those piercing eyes which reminded him so much of his own. Tears flowed uncontrollably as the two men hugged each other.

Amare was crying for the same reasons Zarik was crying and more, since he knew what Zarik would have to endure. Amare traced Zarik's face with his hands; he smelt his hair and kissed his forehead while inhaling deeply, as if to extract the very essence of Zarik's being. He was determined now more than ever to never lose his son again.

As they settled, Zarik told Amare about his two sisters but started to cry again as he mentioned his mother's name. Binta was raped and killed trying to protect her daughters from being captured. The entire village was burnt to the ground, the attackers killing all the elderly folk and taking the young strong men and women. Amare could not contain himself. His eyes were like crimson, his veins could barely contain the pressure within them, and his temperature rose higher than Zarik's was the night before. He felt like he could kill all of the overseers by himself but knew if he didn't compose himself that he would make it worse for Zarik.

Amare choked back tears as he remembered Binta as an astoundingly remarkable woman. She was strong and combative, beautiful and majestic, tumultuous yet calming, purpose-driven and resolute, yet still loving and compassionate.

He thought about the first time he saw the love of his life, Binta. They were both children. She was seven years old and Amare was ten. She really loved playing and would pretend that she was a mother with kids and cooking for them. Amare did not know how to describe what he felt for Binta at that age but he became really shy every time she looked at him. As they got older, he always positioned himself to capture her attention, even though she would ignore him when he behaved silly. He reminisced about the day when he saw a different sparkle in Binta's eyes. She had fallen and cut her leg fairly badly. Amare immediately rushed to her aid as he went deep into the jungle to find some special leaves and placed them on her open wound. He continued to check on her daily until she fully recovered and the scar faded.

Still fighting back his tears, he asked about his daughters. Binta had given birth to two beautiful daughters, Aziza and Zema, who were the spitting image of their mother. Lynch bought both sisters and had them somewhere on the plantation. It was soon time to go to the field so Amare tried to teach Zarik everything he knew to help him get through the day. He also told him not to let anyone know that he was his son, for fear of them being separated or worse.

It was harvest time on the sugar cane plantation, a time that was extremely demanding. Amare and Zarik worked harder than ever. Zarik was weak because he was dehydrated and had lost a lot of blood. Despite his condition, he was still beaten unmercifully. Amare watched and cried hopelessly as he felt every blow Zarik received.

As Amare continued to work, gunshots rang out in the distance, dogs were barking and the air was filled with agonising screams. As Amare turned his head in the direction of the commotion he saw four slaves, two overseers on horseback and three dogs. The slaves were laughing and leaning on one another as if in support of some great accomplishment. The horsemen rode next to each other, with one horseman pulling a carriage containing a slave who was writhing in pain because his legs and arms were severely bitten and resembled minced meat. The dogs' mouths and fur were covered in blood. Later that day Amare found out that the slave that was being carried on the carriage by the horseman died due to his injuries. He had lost a significant amount of blood after he was shot and mauled by the dogs. He had tried to escape during the night and a search party was dispatched to recapture him. As the overseers stood over his dead body, Mr Lynch paid them for their work. This enraged Amare even more.

These devils are *being paid to capture us, to beat us, to guard us and to kill us.* Amare cried out to the God of his forefathers. "Oh God! Why did you create me?! Surely not to endure this suffering from the hands of these evil men! It would have been better if you didn't fashion me from the soil of the earth and allowed me to remain as dirt instead of being treated like dirt. Why, oh God, do you stay silent in the midst of this terror? Why, oh God, have you turned your back on your people, allowing them to be butchered and slain like beasts? Why, oh God, have you covered your eyes? Is it because they're filled with tears as you watch these men rape and kill women and innocent children? Oh God, do you not hear your people crying?! Oh God, how long do we have to beg?! Oh God, don't let us have to beg you as well without relief! We beg the white man to no avail. We beg them to stop the beatings! Stop the beatings, oh God, for as long as there is breath within our bodies, there will be beatings. There will be tearing of my flesh. There will be spilling of my blood. I shudder when I see a raised hand. My bowels get weak when I hear the cracking of the whip. Oh my God, is there no end to this madness?! Oh God, did you not assign my value before I was fashioned from the earth?! Why am I now deemed worthless?! Take me, oh God! Open up the earth and prepare my grave, for I'd rather die than to live another day as a slave!"

Later that night, back in the hut, Amare treated Zarik's wounds and made sure Zarik built his strength quickly by feeding him all the food they were given. He also showed him how to observe and how to behave.

Over the years, Amare never uttered his plans, since he felt like he couldn't trust anyone. He saw how divisive Lynch was by rewarding slaves for telling on each other. Mr Lynch and the overseers also slept with the black slave women, who gave birth to offspring with lighter complexions. The slaves with the lighter complexions would typically receive preferential treatment, creating division between them and their darker-skinned brethren. Lynch then separated the slaves by placing the lighter-skinned slaves to work in the house and the darker-skinned slaves to work in the fields.

It didn't take Amare long to realize that his black brothers were starting to conform. He watched how powerless the slaves seemed, although they outnumbered the overseers. Over time, he saw black overseers eagerly executing their duties by whipping their own brothers with ferocious intent, just to impress. Black men were proud to do massa's bidding while ignoring themselves, like the butcher who didn't even secure a piece of meat for himself, although he was hungry.

Amare now had Zarik with him, someone whom he could trust with his life. Every night they spoke in hushed tones rehearsing their plan of action. They didn't know how big the island was or its terrain. They were usually kept isolated from other slaves and their owners on other plantations. Several slaves in the past who tried to escape were hunted down and brought back. It was rumoured that those who didn't return were killed.

CHAPTER THREE

Breaking Point

As slaves were becoming more expensive to obtain, Lynch decided to use the strong men as bucks to have sex with as many of the black slave girls as possible to breed them.

It was still early and the morning was cool, as the dew hadn't fully evaporated from the leaves that it covered earlier. Amare and Zarik were dragged from the hut and blindfolded, along with several other men. Lynch picked the strongest men and women, who were tall and of good stature.

There were six men chosen to have sex with fourteen women that morning. It had been fifteen years since Amare last had sex and he constantly reminisced about being inside his wife's vagina, which gladly accepted every inch of his sizeable member. It wasn't just the sex; he loved her with every cell in his body.

Every morning Amare would be awakened by the throbbing of his penis. He was as potent as a horse and would have easily been able to perform. However, this morning was different, as he was blindfolded and his daughters didn't know him. He would never be able to live with himself afterwards if he impregnated one of them. The overseers loved watching these acts committed in the open for their perverse pleasure.

Aziza and Zema, knowing the face of their brother Zarik, quickly avoided him and paired up with men they didn't know. Zema ended up pairing with her father Amare, unknowingly. However, since Amare knew that the possibility existed for it to be one of his daughters, he vehemently refused to have sex with anyone and his penis remained flaccid and unresponsive.

An overseer who could not restrain himself anymore after seeing how beautiful Zema was grabbed her by her locks, forced her to the ground and raped her, cursing and beating her as he did it.

Different women were paired with Amare, to no avail. Lynch removed the blindfold from Amare. He then tied him to a tree so Amare could watch how the men behaved as they ravished the women. The other men ejaculated quickly to spread their seed and experience as many women as possible.

This ordeal was not at all pleasurable for the women, as most of them were virgins and had small cavities which remained dry during intercourse due to the lack of intimacy. The men were in no way sympathetic to their cries.

Zarik was heartbroken after seeing Zema being raped but somewhat relieved that he was spared from having sex with either her or Aziza.

Lynch was charged up and felt disrespected by Amare's lack of performance. He ordered the overseers to tie Amare facing the tree, with his bare flesh pressed onto the tree and his legs spread apart. Lynch then sodomized Amare in front of all of the onlookers. Amare begged for mercy; he cried and pleaded with Lynch to stop.

"I broke the will of my buck by breaking his ass!" yelled Lynch at the top of his voice for all to hear. The episode lasted for about two minutes but it felt longer and worse than all the experiences combined over the years for Amare. It was on that tree that Amare finally decided to let his ghost fly and preferred to die than to live another day.

Zarik could not stand to watch the abominable act as it took place but felt his father's agonizing cries. Amare was untied and dropped to the ground with his face inches away from the scattered droplets of semen mingled with dirt and blood. He looked up with his tear-filled eyes and saw Aziza and Zema in the distance. He had never seen them before but seeing them was like seeing Binta. He smiled.

Amare saw boots, a muzzle, the whites of Zarik's eyes, the back of his throat, the veins in his neck, as he tried to reach him but was restrained. Amare felt a cold metal object on his temple; a blast rocked his head—silence, blackness. Amare was dead with a single gunshot to his head.

Zarik was frozen as he watched his father's lifeless body being loaded onto a carriage and wheeled away. He had seen these senseless killings before but this was his father, whom he loved. This was the man he wanted to be like. Although he was only six when they were separated for the first time, his father's spirit lived in him throughout the years. It was a miracle to see him again after so long. Now, he was gone for good, leaving behind only fragments of his flesh and blood to bake in the dust.

There was silence in the air as even the trees seemed to bow, paying respect. Zarik could hardly work that day and was beaten to a pulp. Blood covered his entire body and he could only faintly stand. He knew his father would want him to be strong for his sisters. As he lay in the hut that night, he replayed his father's plans in his head, determined to make them a reality.

CHAPTER FOUR

The Programming

Zarik was gathering hay late one afternoon when he distinctly overheard Mr Lynch talking. He positioned himself closer and looked through a crack in the barn. Mr Lynch was talking to another plantation owner called Mr Yarde, from one of the nearby plantations. Yarde was highly respected by the other plantation owners for how he managed the slaves on his plantation. He ran a tight ship, with a high number of upheavals. However, he was ruthless and known for beating several of his slaves until they died.

"I seem to be losing money with these blasted niggers," said Yarde.

"That is because your approach is wrong. It is very expensive to replace niggers when you kill them before getting your money's worth," Lynch remarked.

"How do you do it, Lynch? Why do your slaves seem to work harder with less supervision?" asked Yarde.

"Well, my strategy is simply a psychological weapon which is pointedly designed to create mistrust and segregation amongst the niggers. So far my strategy is working and proving to be very effective as it places emphasis on the differences between the slaves and uses those differences to cause division," Lynch replied.

"But exactly how?" asked Yarde, eager to hear the response.

"Well, I place the old against the young, the women against the men, the light against the dark, tall against short, fine hair against coarse hair. I told my niggers that they should only trust me and not to trust each other because they will betray each other," Lynch said, smiling.

"I know relationships cannot be formed without trust and communities cannot be formed without relationships. This will make slaves subservient for hundreds of years," continued Lynch while taking a shot of rum.

"Brilliant, Lynch, let us toast to that—niggers divided by design," said Yarde as he held up his glass.

Zarik watched while tears streamed down his face as he wept for past, present and future generations.

Months passed as life on the plantation continued as usual. Both sisters had given birth, Aziza to a beautiful ebony princess called Niru and Zema to a beautiful mulatto princess called Anna. Zema was scared and cried when she saw that Anna was very pale. She thought that Anna was sick since her eyes were greenish in colour and her hair was strange in texture. Zema in time would come to realise that Anna was not sick but highly favoured because of her complexion.

The two cousins loved each other and spent every waking moment in each other's company. However, that abruptly changed when Anna was forbidden from playing with her cousin Niru. They were separated and Anna was moved to a small room in the plantation house, while Niru remained in the hut with her mother and her aunt. It was now Aziza's turn to cry as Niru could not understand why she wasn't allowed to go into the big house to be with her beloved Anna.

One day, as Aziza was plaiting Niru's hair, Niru saw Anna and she darted out of her mother's hands, shouting, "Anna! Anna!" since she had not seen Anna for a while. Anna heard Niru's voice and her eyes lit up when she saw Niru running towards her. Just as Niru was about to embrace Anna, Niru was met with a slap from one of the house slaves that sent Niru skating across the courtyard.

Aziza wailed for her daughter as she lifted her and saw the shape of a hand branded across her swollen cheek. Zema could only watch, feeling hurt and responsible for what occurred. Zema loved her daughter Anna from a distance, as she wasn't allowed to be with her. As the girls grew older, the differences between them became very apparent.

Niru spoke the broken dialect of the slaves. Her clothing was old, tattered, and oversized. Her hair was coarse and matted. She was lean, and her skin was sun-baked from working in the field every day.

Anna, on the other hand, spoke the "Queen's English" and she wore the nicest frilly dresses, with matching hats to cover her long, flowing hair. Her skin seemed unblemished, as she was always in the shelter of the house, never having to endure the sun's rays.

Zarik loved his niece Niru with all of his heart and as she grew older the bond they shared deepened. Zarik also knew that as often as he was used as a buck, he could have daughters he didn't know of and the likelihood of someday being confronted with the same dreaded fate as his father weighed heavily on his heart. He was prepared to die before ever defiling his unknown daughters or his beloved Niru.

Zarik was very observant, as his father had taught him well. He noticed that the slaves who were chosen to be bucks were stronger and seemed to be coping better with being oppressed than the other slaves. They were usually given authority or used to subdue the dissenters. They were bigger in body but seemed weaker and smaller in mind, as they appeared powerless and contented to please massa despite their circumstances.

The bucks were the envy of the black slave men and deemed more valuable than the average slave. They were selected by massa to sow seeds with reckless abandon, to breed and flee. They never experienced the burden of raising children and in many cases didn't even know their children. This opportunity allowed the bucks to empty the contents of their testicular sacs into many vaginas of all shapes, sizes, and ages. This provided a momentary escape of orgasmic pleasure from their perilous reality. The buck with the big dick became an empty, ignorant man governed by his manhood and ruled blindly by his desire for sex.

CHAPTER FIVE

The Plan

Zarik was conflicted as he constantly heard his father's voice in his head, reminding him not to trust anyone. He always obeyed his father while he was alive and didn't want to disobey him now that he was dead. However, Zarik had a decision to make, and he knew that he could not execute the plan alone.

He had unofficially adopted Mali as a father figure ever since Amare was killed. Mali was a towering, powerful man who had lived as a slave on the plantation for about twenty years. The two men had developed a level of camaraderie. Zarik felt as though time was running out and he decided to share his simple but risky plan to finally free himself from the perpetual turmoil.

One night as Zarik was quietly speaking to Mali about the plan, he paused several times to check for eavesdroppers. The plan was to enter the big house in the darkness of the night, while massa was sound asleep, and cut his throat from ear to ear, then burn the house to the ground and head off into the dark with supplies to last them for a few days. As the men spoke, footsteps were heard outside of the hut. Zarik quietly made his way outside and signalled for Mali not to speak. He was quite relieved to see a dog rummaging through the garbage. Zarik was justifiably paranoid, as the level of distrust was sickeningly high, with slaves having more loyalty to massa than to each other. After Zarik re-entered the hut the two men conversed about what Zarik had overheard between Mr Lynch and Mr Yarde. Shaking their heads in disbelief, the two men looked at each other and with very few words decided to execute their plan the following night.

That night, Zarik could hardly sleep as his mind raced. He thought of Aziza, Zema, Niru, and Anna. He thought of where he would go after he escaped, but he didn't have answers for many of the difficult questions that he asked himself. However, he was certain that Lynch had to pay for killing his father and for the years of torment caused to his people by uprooting them from their land, abusing their bodies, and tormenting their souls, all for greed. The black people did not agree of their own free will to work for the white man. Why didn't he, the white man, use his own people in the same way?

The morning took forever but it eventually came. The men worked in the field as smartly as they could, trying their best not to be beaten by the overseers since a good whipping, along with the hard work, could have potentially caused them to abort their plans for later. After work, both Zarik and Mali decided to eat as much as they could have and rested early, to conserve their energy for the task ahead.

That night, both men slept like logs before arising with synchronized timing and preparing themselves without uttering a word, as though they were under the influence of a hypnotic spell. The night was unusually silent, with not even a sound from the crickets or frogs. The air was humid, with hardly any breeze. Outside was a pitch-black, starless sky. Zarik secured the knife he had stolen from the butcher; what a suitable weapon for killing a pig.

The men knew it was now or never. Mali gave Zarik a reassuring look, as if to say everything was going to be okay. The men exited the hut and made their way across the courtyard. When they reached the house, all of the windows were closed except for one on the northern side of the house, which was perfect to reach as it was lower to the ground. This was like a blessing in disguise since prying a window open could have awoken massa. Mali climbed through the window first, while Zarik watched. After Zarik was sure that no one was watching, he made his way inside behind Mali.

This was their first time seeing the inside of the big house. The sights they saw were astonishing and drew a stark comparison to their hut. There were polished wooden floors instead of mud floors and spacious rooms with high ceilings as opposed to cramped living spaces. Bedrooms with nice big beds compared to a piece of plank. The wooden floor, however, was making it difficult to move without a sound.

At the top of the stairs was a big white door. The two men had a gut feeling that Lynch was behind that door. They climbed the stairs as quietly as they could. When they reached the top, Zarik turned the knob. His body was drenched in sweat and his heart was pounding hard, as though it was trying to escape through his skin, so he placed his hand over his chest to prevent his heart from leaving him.

He pushed the door and a screeching, annoyingly loud noise was heard, like a female cat in heat. Zarik paused to look back for

Mali since he could no longer hear or feel the heat from Mali's breath on his neck. He was startled when out of nowhere, he saw two small dots, an inch and a half apart, floating about six feet in the air moving towards him. The dots disappeared then reappeared. As the dots got closer, Zarik breathed a sigh of relief when he realized that they were only Mali's blinking eyes.

The two men eased through the open space. Zarik drew his knife from his waist and walked towards the bed with purpose and intent, ready to drench those white sheets with the blood of the pig. Suddenly a door slammed and another one opened and slammed; footsteps raced up the creaky staircase. Zarik and Mali panicked, as there was nowhere to escape or hide. A flickering light entered the room, revealing the faces of the butcher and Lynch, who was told about the plot against his life the day before. The butcher had seen when Zarik stole the knife and reckoned that Zarik was up to no good so he decided to spy on him. The footsteps Zarik heard outside the hut on the same night that he revealed the plot to Mali were the butcher's footsteps.

Zarik was paralyzed with disbelief. He could not fathom how his plot was exposed by one of his own. By this time, the room was filled with house slaves and overseers with guns. Mali and Zarik, with only a blade in hand, decided to surrender without a struggle.

They were both taken outside. "Mali, how could you betray me like this, after all I have done for you?!" Lynch said as he spat in Mali's face. Mali's vision was momentarily blurred by Lynch's venomous saliva. As he regained his focus, Mali saw his wife and his two young sons a stone's throw away. His wife's cries were drowned out by the braying sounds of horses and their hooves as they were led into the courtyard.

She had cried for Mali before, but tonight was different. Mali was knocked to the ground and ropes were tied to his legs, with each one of his legs being secured to a different horse facing opposite directions. Both horses were then slapped at the same time. Mali was violently ripped in half like a piece of dry, rotted crocus. One horse galloped to the east and the other to the west, with each of the horses dragging a bloody, mangled half of Mali's body as they ran. Mali's wife tried to cover her sons' eyes but it was too late.

The overseers then took turns beating Zarik to the very entrance of death's door. The door would open and as Zarik's spirit tried to enter, the door would slam shut. This continued for a while, as Lynch had given strict orders to not kill Zarik, so as not to lose two slaves that night. Zarik's body was swollen nearly twice its normal size, with blood coming out of his eyes, ears, nose, and mouth.

The rain started to fall and Zarik was left there in the mud that night. As the slaves rose that morning, they could smell the carnage that occurred the night before permeating the air. Niru was the first, however, to see Zarik. She could not hold back her tears as she wailed uncontrollably for her uncle, whom she feared was dead. Aziza and Zema heard Niru and rushed to her side, only to see their brother's outstretched body in a pool of blood, struggling to make a gurgling sound, as though he was choking on his own mucus.

The sisters repositioned their brother's head carefully, so as not to further injure him. Zarik started to breathe heavier and then coughed and farted at the same time, soiling himself. The other slaves watched as the ladies struggled with Zarik. Anna was passing by at this time and saw what was going on but deliberately positioned herself to appear as though she hadn't seen.

Zarik's condition continued to deteriorate, as the blows he had received broke his ribs and punctured his lungs, making it extremely difficult for him to breathe. Aziza and Zema tried their best to stay with him but were ordered to work in the fields, leaving Zarik alone and without care. Zarik would drift in and out of consciousness, as he wasn't getting enough oxygen. He couldn't help himself and relied totally on his sisters' assistance.

As Zarik lay in the hot, dusty hut, Lynch passed by and looked in. "This nigger is costing me more alive than dead," said Lynch. He then took hold of Zarik's leg and proceeded to drag him out of the hut.

As he was about to exit Niru entered. "Oh no!" she screamed. "Leave Zarik alone!" Niru was usually soft-spoken and timid, but Zarik was her hero and it broke her heart to see him treated in this way.

Lynch, enraged and surprised that he was spoken to like that, yanked Niru farther inside the hut. He released Zarik's leg and placed his filthy hands over Niru's mouth as she fought bitterly. His focus was now on defiling her innocence. She had never been touched by a man before and started to quiver when she saw the lust in his eyes. He groped her young, perky breasts with his hands, while breathing heavily down her neck. Niru struggled but she was no match for him. He forced her to the ground and clumsily had his way with her.

Zarik watched helplessly as tears flowed down his cheeks. As soon as Lynch was finished he pulled up his pants and hurriedly left the hut. Niru, writhing in pain, struggled to crawl over to Zarik and placed her head on her uncle's shoulder for comfort.

Later that evening when Aziza and Zema returned to the hut from a really hard day in the field, they saw Niru crying and thought that their brother Zarik was dead for sure. However, they were confronted with the blatant and disgusting evidence of Niru's stolen innocence. That night pain and anguish filled their hut.

CHAPTER SIX

Lost Men

In the morning Zarik's gaze was fixed; his body was rigid, as though frozen solid. Aziza placed her hand on his head and his skin felt cold. "Zarik!" she shouted. "Oh my God!" Zarik was dead. He was a strong man but had lost the battle when Niru was raped. Moments later, like clockwork, the overseers came to summon the ladies for work after hearing the commotion.

On recognizing that Zarik was dead, two slaves dragged his lifeless body out of the hut and threw it onto a cart. Those same slaves ignored the deafening wails of the women and forcibly ushered them off to the fields to start the day's work.

As the months passed and Niru became visibly pregnant, the expectant mother, instead of being filled with joy, wanted to rid herself of the devil's offspring. Still herself a child and not knowing how to cope or what to expect, she leaned even more on her mother.

It was a Tuesday around eleven in the morning when Niru's water broke while she was in the field. Luckily, Aziza was close by when it happened. The contractions were fierce and frequent and the scorching sun was relentless. No sooner had Aziza cleared a patch in the shade and Zema arrived with the water and cloth, than Niru was on her back, pushing and screaming, while squeezing her mother's hand to a pulp. For Aziza, the loss of feeling in her hand was a small price to pay, knowing the physical and psychological turmoil her daughter was experiencing.

Niru wanted the baby out of her. For nine months, it felt like a cancerous tumour. She knew as soon as the baby was born, she would be separated from it, hopefully never to see it again. Niru bore the teeth-grinding, excruciating pain as she watched the big head of the bastard baby stretch her privates to the limit. Despite the indescribable pain she had never experienced before, Niru continued to push. The baby's cries soon filled the air. Niru had given birth to a son. Her hardened heart melted instantly when she laid eyes on him. He wasn't pale like the demon who killed her soul or black like her. He was brown and his features reminded her of Zarik.

Aziza and Zema took Niru back to the hut to clean her up. Niru was weak, exhausted and could hardly keep her eyes open, so the sisters left her as she rested with her newborn. She was awakened by his cries of hunger after a few hours and drew him closer to her, placing her swollen breast filled with milk in his mouth. He instantly stopped crying as his tiny mouth was filled. Niru watched her son and in her mind named him Zarik, as all of the slaves and their offspring were being slowly but surely stripped of their original names.

As she lay there bonding with her son, Lynch entered the hut. Niru was crippled with fear when she saw him. She cried as she thought that Lynch was going to harm her baby or rape her again. Lynch, on seeing the baby, was surprised by its appearance but relieved at the same time, since it didn't resemble him. He could now quell his mistress' wrath by craftily discrediting what she had heard as nothing but wicked and malicious rumours. "Call this nigger Darnley," he said as he spat in her face and left the hut. Oh, how she wanted to kill Lynch! Oh, how she wanted to watch his blood slowly drain from his body, burying him alive in a grave filled with shit and urine. The hatred was real.

CHAPTER SEVEN

The Black Woman's Resolve

Niru at this point was only fourteen years old but she was a quick learner. Her maternal instincts kicked in during the month that she was allowed to rest. Niru, although young and impressionable, still reacted like most of the older women who would have suffered similar traumatic experiences. She became totally submissive in her attempt to protect herself and her son by being as obedient as possible, so as not to anger the overseers or Lynch, for fear of what they would do to them.

Black slave women always worked hard while lovingly submitting to their husbands. Black slave women were always placed in a very precarious position of having their men, their protectors, their providers, their lovers, the heads of their households, yanked from the body of their family by the white man. A body is no use without the head and the head is no use without the body. Together they provided the ideal environment for their children to grow and succeed, and without each other, the entire family would rot and decay.

Not only were these black women supposed to live with their heads ripped off but they were expected to serve new heads, white heads, now positioned on their black bodies—the making of hideous monsters. The pain of black women having to open their legs willingly or by force to give their very essence to white beasts was a pain to which not even the tearing of flesh by whips could compare.

Years passed and the white beast, the blasted pig, Mr Lynch, was finally dead. God allows the rain to fall on the just and the unjust. It almost seemed like God was unjust to let this vile hog traverse the land for so long, leaving a legacy of death, destruction, and pain. It seemed like God was unjust to allow Lynch's putrid spirit to simply exit his body as he slept. This pig of a man should have been carved into many pieces by all those he hurt and his rancid meat fed to the dogs, which would have surely refused it. The heavens rejoiced that morning as the black clouds which seemed to represent all the black slaves Lynch killed in the past could not contain themselves and shed tears of joy to cleanse the land. Lynch's death was like closing a chapter in Niru's life which represented so much pain. He had devastated her life by killing her grandfather and her uncle, and raping her.

It seemed like only yesterday that Niru had given birth to Darnley in the field. After a couple of months, he was already alert and strapped to her back while she toiled in the sun, only pausing briefly to breastfeed him. As he continued to grow, there was no shortage of love showered upon Darnley from his mother, his grandmother, and his aunt. Niru had to be strong and be both a mother and a father to Darnley but how could she be when she never had a father herself? All of the strong men that she could have possibly learned from were either dead or broken. She tried her best but it was hard raising a boy without a father, while still working her ass off on the plantation.

As Darnley got older he never knew or asked about his father, as it was normal for most of the black boys to be fatherless. Darnley's case wasn't unique but his father's identity had to be kept a secret, even though his father was dead. Darnley had absolutely no male figures in his life and Niru wished she had a partner who would help her to raise Darnley. The slave men she entertained, however, had no sense of duty to family and were only focussed on repositioning her womb. It was hard for Darnley not to notice the cavalier attitude with which the men dealt with his mother. She was by no means a whore but the trial and error racked up the number of men she encountered, which had an adverse impact on Darnley's attitude to women as he became older.

Darnley developed an unquenchable fascination for women and, not having a father figure, he gravitated to the bucks since the bucks seemed to be more confident than the other slaves. Over the years he tried to qualify his intrigue for women, which he thought was just the natural curiosity that existed between the two sexes. Noticing his delinquency, Niru constantly chastised Darnley, who in turn became repulsed by her incessant bickering. Feelings of resentment overshadowed every act of kindness she exhibited towards him. He no longer saw his mother's sacrifice as a labour of love but more as her duty and became extremely rebellious and disrespectful to her.

Niru started to question if something was wrong with herself, given that no man wanted to claim her as his own. She fully understood the stress of being in a relationship on the plantation; however, she was still eager. Insecure men exploited her, although she was sweet and submissive. These men, probably in their quest to regain some semblance of authority, chose to lord over Niru instead of loving her. Niru was not only being treated as a slave by massa, she was now also being treated as a slave by the black men she loved instead of being treated as their equal and queen. Over the years she grew to despise the very ground these men walked on.

CHAPTER EIGHT

The Evolution

This pear-shaped island called Barbados basked in the sun daily while she bathed in the Atlantic Ocean, with its waters teasingly caressing her boundaries. She was always beautifully adorned in a cascading green dress which trailed for miles, hugging her contours and complemented by an array of colourful accessories. She was innocent like a fertile virgin, full of life to offer. This virgin was held captive, raped for centuries and abandoned like her mother Africa and several of her sisters across the ocean. Her supple breasts were greedily drained of their nutrients by a few white strangers and their offspring, growing in stature, while they stood on her black children, breaking their backs with their increasingly burdensome weight for nearly four hundred years.

Over time, there was life and growth, death and decay. Like a caterpillar metamorphosises into a butterfly, so transformed the island's inhabitants and all contained within.

Nature dictates that the old should pass to make way for the new. So should the passing of many moons to usher in a new dispensation. The new was being built on the old guard in the form of Amare, Zarik, Aziza, Zema, Niru, Darnley, and their descendants who, with their blood, sweat, and tears, gradually transformed the landscape of the island over the years.

Undefined primitive tracks, carved after years of constant trodding by beast and man, were replaced by well-defined networks of paved highways. Mud huts with thatched roofs were replaced by chattel houses on tenantry land and massive brick houses in the heights and terraces. For every parish church, there were twice as many rum shops. The village shops were replaced by supermarkets. Sugar plantations once used to cultivate crops were now used for industrial and housing developments. From revolutions to independence to changes in politics, commerce and culture. Titles changed from massa to business owner as the white man continued to prosper and from slave to labourer as poverty, one of the many by-products of slavery, continued to plague the black man.

PART TWO

CHAPTER NINE

A New Era

"Susan, you need to get up and get your little ass ready for school! Your father does not support us, and I just cannot afford to lose my job!" Susan's mother Velma bellowed loudly. Susan and Velma Lynch were descendents of Niru and had inherited their surname from Lynch, the wicked plantation owner who had killed Amare and their other ancestors. Velma was a beautiful, dark brown woman in her mid-twenties. She was seventeen years of age when she had her daughter Susan. Velma was very poor and worked long and hard for virtually no pay for Mr Williams, who was a wealthy, white Bajan man who owned a big supermarket chain in the city. Susan only knew her father by his nickname, "Starboy." He was a notorious village ram who had eleven children from ten different women. Susan would only see him when he visited the house to petition her mother for sex or money.

The Lynches lived on tenantry land left to them by Velma's grandmother, who died when Velma was eighteen. Velma's grandmother had worked on the sugar plantation for many years cutting cane. The tenantry land was located in a densely populated village, with no clear landmarks or divisions between the houses. The yards were small and dusty, with yard fowls searching aimlessly for scraps while Benjamin, the village cock, kept a vigilant eye as he strutted proudly. Most of the neighbours were extended family that lived extremely close to each other, with absolutely no privacy. The house was a single-room, termite-infested chattel house which balanced on loosely stacked stones.

There was no indoor plumbing and water was usually fetched from the standpipe for bathing and cooking. The toilet was situated over a pit and enclosed in a galvanized structure a couple meters away from the house. At night, Susan and Velma would use a metal potty, since they were afraid of their own shadows, which seemed like monsters in the dark. It was virtually impossible for the two of them to share the chink-filled single mattress in their cramped living space but they tried.

Susan would be awakened by gripping hunger pangs every morning, despite drinking lots of water to act as a buffer to prevent her stomach from touching her back. She knew the menu by heart and would eagerly await breakfast, which always consisted of a combination of sugar, flour and grease. Today, Susan could not wait as Velma prepared Susan's favourite, cornmeal pap and bakes. Susan almost fell out of her chair when Velma surprised her by also frying an egg which she found under the cellar.

After breakfast, Susan made the two-mile trek to school through a rocky track next to Mr Williams' property. She couldn't help but notice the contrast to her own home. There were endless acres of beautifully landscaped, cascading lawns and a huge, skilfully-designed automated iron gate. The gate provided a veil of privacy, concealing the long driveway which was flanked by towering palm trees leading to a massive, perfectly appointed two-story mansion, with large patios and French doors.

Some days while making her daily trek, she would pause and marvel at the movement of the gate as it opened, allowing her fantasizing stares to trespass. Her dream to someday own a similar property, along with her mother's encouragement, fuelled her fire to excel at school.

CHAPTER TEN

The Colour Black

B lack bitch, tar-baby, golliwog, blackbird," teased a girl as soon as Susan entered her classroom. School was hard, as she was constantly bullied and taunted by her schoolmates about her complexion. Daily they would remind her of how black and greasy she was.

At the tender age of seven, she could not fathom what she had done to deserve the onslaught of insults hurled in her direction from persons who looked just like her. Susan would cry until her eyes were red and swollen. She would become congested and choked up, trying feverishly to wipe away the mucous which would stream out of her nostrils. The children would erupt with laughter and jeer her even more.

As she got older and entered senior school, it got worse. It was ironic that the children with lighter skin tones hardly made fun of her. However, darker children always did. How was this even possible, that in a class filled with only blacks no one wanted to be the blackest? No one wanted to be her friend. Sometimes she would have feelings of anger and resentment towards Starboy her father for being so black, broke and whoring. Sometimes she wished that her mother was a lighter complexion.

At sixteen years old, Susan was a naturally brilliant student. However, this constant bashing was starting to take a toll on her grades. Her self-esteem was shattered and she never looked people directly in their eyes because she felt ugly.

During lunch one day, while Susan was in the bathroom crying, as usual, Tyra, a brown-skinned girl, approached her and gave her a container of skin bleaching cream. Susan was doubly shocked, as no one had ever approached her or given her anything at school before. Tyra told Susan to read the instructions and hurriedly left the bathroom, so as not to be seen with her.

Susan entered one of the stalls, closed the door, sat on the toilet with the lid down, and read the instructions. She was an avid reader and very proficient in the English language. However, she struggled while reading the instructions and ingredients, as she could not pronounce or understand most of the words since they were lengthy and scientific in origin. The harmful side effects were numerous but paled in comparison to the prospect of finally becoming white.

That evening, she raced home to apply the cream to her face before her mother got there. She was eager because she felt that this was going to be her saviour. She finally was going to be rid of this black skin which she despised so much and for which she didn't ask. She applied the cream as instructed and searched hopelessly for somewhere to hide the container before her mother got home. Her efforts were futile, so she kept it in her bag.

That night trying to focus on her homework was very challenging, as she kept daydreaming about her new appearance and friends. Susan deliberately went to bed after her mother and avoided facing her while sleeping since she was certain Velma would smell the cream on her face and ask about it.

The next morning Susan rose first, eager to see results in the mirror. She was disappointed when confronted by the same black face. The instructions on the container said to expect visible changes within a week, which seemed too long to wait. She thought if she increased the amount of cream and the applications that she would see results even faster.

For the next few days, Susan became totally consumed with her new agenda. She would apply the cream morning, noon, and night. Her face would burn as her perspiration felt like acid oozing from her pores. However, this was a small price to pay as she thought that the burning sensation was confirmation of the cream working.

One morning, Susan awoke and went to the mirror as accustomed. She was overjoyed and whispered excitedly, "Oh my God!" as her black hand covered her brown mouth. After she calmed down, realization struck her. She was easily able to hide the container from her mother but where and how was she going to hide her new face? She cycled through a range of emotions while preparing for her mother's questions.

Susan reached over her mother as she slept to remove the soiled white pillow case blackened by her old face while trying her best not to touch her mother. However, she did. Loud screams drowned out the sounds of the crowing roosters, as Velma panicked. "Mum, Mum, it's me!"

"Oh my God, Susan! What did you do to your skin?!" shouted Velma as she looked at her daughter's face, which was now a two-toned collage of confusion—the lighter tone where Susan had applied the cream and the original black tone around her eyes, lips, ears, and hairline, where the cream was evidently not applied.

They argued that morning, with Velma demanding to see the container. "Where did you get this from?!" yelled Velma as she opened the empty container. Velma knew that Susan couldn't have afforded the cream since Velma was barely able to give Susan money for lunch.

Velma's anger quickly turned to sadness and compassion as Susan shouted at the top of her lungs, "I hate God! Why did he have to make me so black?!"

It was then that Velma truly felt the mental anguish of her daughter. Velma embraced Susan, gently kissed her face, wiped her tears and softly whispered, "I love you."

The two ladies composed themselves, as it was getting late, and prepared to head off in their different directions. Susan went to school with her head held high that morning. The argument with her mother did not faze or derail her.

It was amazing to see what a few patches of brown skin did to raise her confidence level. However, that confidence was shattered immediately as she entered the classroom. The children made mooing sounds and called her a cow. They joked non-stop. The insults were fast and vicious.

When Tyra initially saw Susan, she chuckled but felt conflicted soon afterwards because trying to help her had made the situation worse. Susan stormed out of the class, totally devastated by this dilemma. She had thought that she would be accepted but she wasn't and she didn't want to return to her former unblemished black tone. She was trapped in her skin by her skin.

Susan knew that applying the cream to the darker areas on her body would eventually even her skin out, so she reached out to Tyra for assistance. However, Tyra could not help since she had only secured that one container from being thrown out at home. Tyra was brown-skinned but had an intimate appreciation of Susan's plight since Tyra had a darker-skinned sister named Shana. Tyra was younger than Shana and remembered being treated differently by their family members, who would all say how pretty Tyra's skin was. On the other hand, they would make fun of Shana. Tyra would get the better gifts for her birthdays and other special occasions. However, Shana's gifts, if she was lucky to get any, would always be an afterthought.

As Tyra and Shana got older, Shana would always tell guys that they would probably prefer Tyra because she was prettier. Ironically, Tyra initially never thought that she was prettier than Shana. She had always secretly admired her sister's rich ebony hue. Shana would be ignored by the guys, who would only look at her as a last resort. After a while, Shana crumbled under the pressure.

Shana tried every product on the shelves, and there were many. Shana did everything to change her appearance. She stole money from her parents and slept with men for money to buy her weaves and expensive wigs. It was only a matter of time before Shana got pregnant, as she was having unprotected sex and not using birth control. She was very lucky not to have contracted HIV. The father of her unborn child pressured her to have an abortion since he already had a girlfriend. Shana, however, decided to keep her child. When the child was born it triggered something in Shana, as the child was black as night. What was she supposed to do now? Drown the baby in bleach to change its complexion? It just didn't make sense anymore.

As the days passed, Susan would not eat and had lost considerable weight. She was depressed and cried uncontrollably as she saw the brownness leaving her face. Every night Velma would watch Susan cry herself to sleep. Exams were rapidly approaching, and Susan had fallen behind significantly with her studies, as she had been absent for several of her classes.

It was six one morning when Velma got ready for work as usual and nudged Susan to prepare for school, but Susan only shrugged her shoulders and pulled the covers over her head. Velma left the house that morning with a heavy spirit and while on the bus travelling to work, she could not stop thinking about Susan.

As she was going to punch her time card, Mr Williams was right there to reprimand and remind her of another time that she was five minutes late. "I will have to deduct this from your pay. There are people lining up for your job."

Velma was a model employee and was only late twice in thirteen years. She usually got to work an hour early and would sometimes skip lunch and work after hours, if necessary. She never complained, although her wages were never raised.

She saw Mr Williams' lips moving but she heard Susan's cries. Everyone at work knew that Velma had it hard. She was uneducated, simple in speech and wore the same old outfits week after week.

Velma rushed to the locker room as tears streamed down her face. She worked in constant fear of losing her job, always being threatened by Mr Williams or one of his supervisors. As she cried, Yvette Maynard, who had overheard the conversation between Velma and Mr Williams, entered the locker room. "Five minutes, Velma! You are always early! Is he for real? Does Mr Williams ever stop to consider your life? Do these white, rich employers ever study the lives of their poor, black employees who work tirelessly to keep their businesses open?"

"Well, I guess it's his business and he can do whatever he wants," Velma said softly, while drying her tears.

"Yes, the business is his investment and by all rights he should get returns. Yes, it's his brainchild and he should do everything within his power to make sure it grows, but that doesn't give him the right to exploit you," said Yvette. "Does he even see when you go above and beyond, working overtime for no pay? Does he know how far you have to walk just to catch a bus? Does he consider that the shit he pays you cannot support you or Susan?"

"You are right 'cause there is barely any money left to buy food after the bills are paid," Velma cried.

"He can, however, find thousands to buy another Jeep to drive to work in air-conditioned comfort, while you can hardly find coins to be packed in a hot-ass bus like sardines in a can," Yvette said as the ladies left the locker room.

Later that day while Velma was arranging the stock in the storeroom, she came across boxes of bleaching cream. Knowing that she didn't have the money to buy them and her request to take them on credit would be denied, she purposed within her heart to steal a few boxes, assuming that she would never be found out. She wrestled with the thought for a while, then she gave in and placed two of the small containers of bleaching cream under her skirt.

As her shift ended and she was preparing to leave, she heard Mr Williams calling her name. She froze and was visibly shaken as buckets of sweat poured down her back. "Velma, make sure you get here early tomorrow or else," he said.

"Yes, Mr Williams, sir," she said nervously as she headed for the door.

When Velma reached home, Susan was still in bed crying. Now fully convinced, Velma took one of the containers of bleaching cream and placed it next to Susan's face. "Oh Mommy, Mommy, I love you!" Susan exclaimed as she sprang up and headed for the mirror. This time she was careful to apply the cream to all of the exposed areas she had neglected before.

Velma felt guilty as hell for what she did but was comforted by her daughter's smiles. After several days of staying indoors and administering the cream, Susan finally got it right. All of the exposed areas of her body that were darker before, including her hands, legs, and neck, were now the same lighter tone.

She had accomplished her goal. She was now a brown-skinned chick. Velma also brought home a do-it-yourself hair relaxer kit, which Susan experimented with over the weekend. By Sunday evening, Susan was totally transformed by her new caramel skin and weakened, long, straightened hair. She could not pull herself away from the mirror that night.

The next day, when she entered the school yard, the response was totally different. The girls were silent; the boys were tapping each other and silently wishing that they had not been so harsh to her. Everyone knew that she had obviously bleached her skin. However, it seemed more acceptable among her peers for her to have done that than to remain the blackest.

For the first time she felt accepted. People were approaching her, touching her hair and asking her about her complexion. She was on top of the world. She was even asked to pose for the cover of the school's magazine, which had specifically asked for light-skinned girls, as it was too much work to prepare lighting and makeup for dark-skinned girls. The darker girls who didn't bleach as yet used filters on their mobile phones to appear lighter, distancing themselves from their reality even if just for a moment.

Months passed and Susan's grades improved. She had done well in her exams and had recently entered college. She was now one of the more popular girls and found herself insulting black-skinned girls although her skin colour was just as black beneath her vest.

Velma continued stealing bleaching cream to support Susan's obsession. However, one day when she was just about to leave work, Yvette Maynard hurriedly entered the locker room with Mr

Rodney D. Lewis

Williams and forcefully snatched Velma's bag. "Look, Mr
Williams, sir, I told you that she was a blasted thief," Yvette said
with a smirk, as though she had saved the day by exposing the
culprit. Yvette's behaviour was totally unexpected and shocked
Velma, as Velma considered Yvette her friend. However, Yvette
was hoping to fill a recent vacancy for a supervisory position and
wanted to impress Mr Williams at any cost. Velma was caught
red-handed with four containers in her bag.

"How could you do this to me after all I did for you?" Mr
Williams asked as he fired Velma on the spot. Velma felt as
though she had heard those words before.

That evening as Velma stood by the bus stop pondering her next
move, Starboy drove up and offered her a ride home in his new
car, which he was very excited about. Velma was choked up and
started crying as she told him that she was fired. However, he
didn't seem to care, as he started telling her about his new car.

Moments later as he pulled into the village, he drove very slowly,
as though he wanted to be seen, speaking to everyone on the
road. Men were hailing him, reaching into the car to give him
high fives. Starboy was just a worthless piece of shit, totally self-
absorbed. He was like several other misdirected black men who
were all about appearances. Black men seemed to like showing
off, displaying everything for the world to see. Here was Starboy
with his new ride decked with the rims and accessories, rolling
in like a celebrity. He was the talk of the town. Oh yes, he was!

"You saw Starboy's new car?" said one of the guys on the block.

"That jackass bought a new car? He can't even support his children, or buy groceries—always begging for money and bought a car?!" exclaimed Latoya Maynard, the daughter of Yvette Maynard.

"That pissy old goat—he is a blasted village ram! Forty-five years old and still living at his mother's house, which is in desperate need of repair. The windows are broken, the wood is rotten and the roof is leaking," she continued.

When Starboy and Velma arrived at Velma's home, Starboy switched off the ignition, locked his car and waited for her to unlock the front door. He stepped inside and started to remove his pants as Velma struggled to keep the door open while holding her bags. As soon as she got inside, he pulled her towards him. "Starboy, I don't..." she started but was abruptly cut off by him silencing her and reminding her that Susan would soon be home.

She had a soft spot for Starboy but this time she felt dirty and unappreciated. He never asked her why she was fired or even tried to console her. He did absolutely nothing at all to make her feel special and behaved as though he was on a timer.

Velma tried to hold back the tears as Starboy relieved himself. As he grunted and groaned, his eyes rolled back, his member became limp, and his body was like a sack of potatoes as he slumped over her. Starboy was dead to the world as he snored like a freight train, causing the house to vibrate. He suddenly arose from his slumber and reached for his faded, stretched-out, crotchless underwear. He got dressed in a flash, zipped up his pants and threw two dollars at Velma. "That should help with Susan's bus fare," he said while leaving.

Velma lay there with only her top on and watched the money as it floated through the air and landed next to her underwear. "Two dollars?" said Velma to herself. She wasn't sure what hurt her more, the money or how Starboy continued to make her feel like trash.

As Velma lay on the ground, she bitterly thought to herself, *Men are dogs because women allow them to be. Men were not designed to be dogs but they became ravenous beasts looking to hunt and devour meat to satisfy their hunger. They only rest from their conquest to feed again. Weak women continue to shape these men by willingly offering themselves. Women say and accept to their own detriment that men have no discipline, first weakening themselves to become willing sacrifices and not understanding that a man who lacks commitment could never satisfy his hunger with only one vagina. Women then get upset when they are used and discarded like trash. A man is designed to enter, and a woman designed to accept. Anything that enters a body has the power to overwhelm that body and leave without being affected. Some women continue to allow toxic men into their lives, who invariably cause damage and destruction when they exit.*

Velma was very beautiful and men flirted with her every day. She, however, committed her life to Starboy although they weren't married. She didn't just want sex; she wanted a family, someone to be there for herself and Susan, and therefore remained foolishly hopeful.

Velma decided not to tell Susan that she had been fired and prepared for work the next day as usual. She knocked on several doors that day in search of a job. She continued this routine for a while and would be offered odd jobs as a housekeeper or porter but didn't receive anything substantial, and her bills had to be paid.

Desperate times called for desperate measures and so, one morning around one-thirty, after ensuring that Susan was fast asleep, Velma got dressed, placed a garbage bag in her pants and left the house as quietly as possible. Outside was cold and damp, as the rain had just fallen. As she walked her eyes lit up, as the street appeared to be lined with gold. Empty plastic bottles were everywhere, as a street party had ended hours earlier. As Velma collected the bottles, it became apparent that she would need several more garbage bags. She hurriedly made her way home with her treasure, which she hid in the backyard before entering the house to get more bags. However, when she entered the house, the rain started to pour and Susan began to stir at the sound of the thunder. Velma reluctantly decided to retire to her bed for a restless night.

Later that day, after Susan left for school, Velma took the bottles to the recycling depot. The bag was filled to the brim and bursting at the seams. She was sure that she would be paid well. However, after all of her hard work, she was only paid five dollars. She was disappointed but convinced herself that a little with contentment was great gain.

The following morning Velma was back on her mission. This time she took several jumbo garbage bags so as not to repeat her mistake from the previous morning. This time she was hardly able to fill one bag, as the same area was nearly already cleared.

Velma had to rummage through several bins and gutters that night to fill two garbage bags. She returned home smelling like filth and decided to rinse the stench off using the pipe in the backyard.

Hiding her bags as she had become accustomed, Velma then sank into her bed to relieve herself of the burdens of the long night and day before. Like clockwork, Velma waited for Susan to leave before rushing to where she hid the bags. However, both bags were gone. Velma stood gazing at the empty space and as reality slowly sank in, she realized that she had done all of that blasted hard work for nothing.

Velma cried. She could not believe it. She needed that money. "Absolutely nobody ever steals from the white man," she said aloud. Hearing herself, she recalled how she stole the bleaching cream from Mr. Williams. "That is different; he had more than enough and was paying me shit for years," Velma replied audibly to her thoughts. She pulled herself together and didn't allow the episode to deter her. She continued on her mission for days, making as much as twenty dollars some mornings, as she was careful to secure her bottles. The money allowed her to pay the water bill, as it was due for disconnection.

Velma found it increasingly difficult to meet her bottle collection quota as other people started collecting bottles in the same area and arriving before her. She realized that for her to make money she would have to find a new location. She saw this competitive trait often with the coconut vendors, who would set up shop only feet away from each other on the highway and fight for the same customers. She didn't want to venture too far from home since she was alone and especially as a woman she had to be careful. One night, she had no choice, as there was absolutely no money to be made in her usual location. Having left home earlier than normal, she decided to try another location a bit farther from her home.

As Velma walked she saw prostitutes on the corner. Some wore nice, lacy lingerie. Others wore thongs and heels, while others were totally naked. They were beautiful young women of all shapes and sizes, some quiet and timid and some loud and boisterous. The ladies were different in many ways but unified in purpose to get the paper.

The night was fairly chilly; Velma was fully clothed and wished that she had worn a thicker shirt. However, these scantily clad women were committed to their trade, as some drivers slowed their cars to window shop and others to take their pick. Velma was not the judgemental type who would be quick to say that these women had other options. She knew that these women were not just standing outside in the cold because they wanted to but because they were desperate and their backs were up against the wall.

"Hi there, sweet girl, do you want some action or are you just watching?" asked a gorgeous twenty-four-year-old Jamaican prostitute named Candy while pressing her breasts together and licking her own nipples.

"No," replied Velma, "I am fine. I just came out to collect bottles."

"Bottles?! A beautiful darkie like you collecting bottles!" exclaimed Candy in her strong Jamaican accent. "I make more from these thirsty men in five minutes than you would in a week," Candy continued.

"Wow! Are you serious?! But isn't it risky?" asked Velma.

"It is, but life is really hard and unfair at times on this island," said Candy. "I am tired of black men. All they see is a pretty face, and they just want sex. They have no intention of being involved.

"What's worse is that they pretend to care and some become possessive, although the cheating bastards have girlfriends and wives at home.

"And what is in it for me?" she asked. "After they get off I still have my bills to pay and my child to feed. This way I keep it simple. We both get what we want without the stress," she continued.

A blue sedan pulled up; the driver let the heavily tinted windows down slightly.

"Hey babe, are you free or are you done for the night?" asked the driver, who was obviously very familiar with Candy.

"Free? I am never free and you know that, Clarkey," Candy said, smiling as she hopped in the car and drove off with the man.

Velma watched the car as it drove farther along, turned off the road, and parked between two trees. The driver turned the lights off, rendering the area pitch black as there were no street lights. Five minutes later, as Velma collected bottles she heard the sound of a car door being closed as the driver turned on his lights and sped off. Velma was certain she had seen that car before, and the driver's voice was also very familiar.

Velma had only collected about fifteen bottles since she didn't have any gloves and scornfully used a stick to remove used condoms off the bottles she had found. As Velma was reaching for another bottle, she heard Candy singing, "Money, money, money, money," as she waved three crisp hundred dollar bills in Velma's face. Velma couldn't believe her eyes. "He lasted long tonight," Candy said while laughing. "Old, dirty, married man. You should have heard him shouting, 'Oh God!' as though he was on the pulpit," joked Candy.

The rain started to fall and Velma decided to call it a night, as she had lost track of time and had to walk farther to get home. Arriving home drenched in sweat and water, Velma continued with her routine and hid the half-filled bag of bottles before sneaking into the house.

Upon entering the house, she was relieved to see that Susan was fast asleep. Velma watched her for a moment and she prayed that God would provide for them, as they had nowhere else to turn.

The following day as she exited the shower, Velma heard a knock at her door. Quickly covering herself with a towel, she opened the door and saw Mr Clarke, a well-respected deacon, who had previously worked for Mr Williams as a supervisor. Velma was happy to see him, as he and his family were always nice to her. Mr Clarke had three sons from his wife of twenty-five years, Mrs Clarke. Despite being glad to see him, she felt exposed before the deacon and God, as her body was only covered by a towel and her house was untidy.

"I heard you were looking for a job and my wife and I would love some assistance around the house. We can't pay you much but the wages should assist in paying your bills," he said, while looking at his watch as if in a hurry.

"Definitely! When can I start?" Velma asked.

"Tomorrow around eight in the morning should be fine," he replied.

As he reached out to give her a hug, she turned her body to the side since she was still holding the towel, but he angled her body to face his and pulled her into him by the small of her back. She felt his erect penis throbbing on her thigh as his breathing got heavier. He kept his right hand in the small of her back while he stepped into the house, keeping her pressed against him as he closed the door with his left hand.

She felt his body shudder and at the same time, her exposed thigh felt wet and sticky. "I only came inside because I would not want an innocent hug to become the next village rumour. I will see you tomorrow," he said and gave her fifty dollars before leaving. Velma was confused and did not know what to make of Mr Clarke's actions. She was also extremely grateful for the money, as she was flat broke and needed money for Susan.

The next morning, Velma showed up at the Clarkes' as planned and was greeted by the warmest smile from Mrs Clarke as she welcomed Velma into her home. At the entrance, there was a life-sized portrait of Mrs Clarke in her twenties when she first met Mr Clarke. She was stunning, brown in complexion, slim and very shapely, with long curly hair. Now, at fifty-one, Mrs Clarke was very sizeable as she had gained considerable weight after giving birth to her youngest son Caleb.

Mrs Clarke gave Velma a quick tour, followed by a list of tasks, and hurried off to work, as she was late. Velma was so happy to be working that she sang at the top of her lungs as she cleaned the Clarke's house. The pay wasn't much but it was better than nothing. She also enjoyed being able to work at her own pace, without interruption.

As she marvelled at how nice the Clarkes' house was and how mannerly their children were, she began to daydream about herself, Starboy, and Susan being a family. Her fantasizing was cut short by the sound of a slamming door, which startled her. Her nerves were quickly quietened when she realized that it was just Mr Clarke, who was seemingly in a hurry. "Is everything ok, sir? Did you forget something?"

"Yes, Velma my love, I think I left my wallet on the counter in my bedroom. Did you see it while you were cleaning?"

"I can't remember but I will check." She hurriedly made her way up the stairs to the master bedroom. Velma searched feverishly for Mr Clarke's wallet. She thought she finally saw it between the lamp and the bed and stretched as far as she could, arching her back while she tried to reach it with her fingers. Mr Clarke entered the room and saw that Velma's skirt had risen up, exposing her perfectly formed apple bottom and the pink lace panty which snugly fit the contours of her pronounced vagina, which was ever so accessible and inviting because of how she was positioned on his bed.

His head felt as though it would explode, as this was the most titillating display of eroticism that he had seen on his bed for nearly twenty-five years. As he gazed for what seemed like an eternity, he tried with all his might to combat what was before him by reflecting on his wife. However, it was a futile exercise as the boring missionary position could never compare with the back-shot from this beautiful black damsel nearly eleven years his wife's junior.

"Mr Clarke, here is your wallet," Velma said to an astonished Mr Clarke, who still had the image of her ass etched in his head and was surprised to see her standing next to him.

Mr Clarke took the wallet and hurriedly left the house. As Velma watched the blue car with the darkly tinted windows quickly drive off, it suddenly hit her that she had seen that car the previous night. Everything about the night came rushing back to Velma. *Oh my God, Mr Clarke is living a lie. He is a cheat and a hypocrite.*

For weeks as Velma worked she became increasingly disgruntled. She had a secret that she couldn't reveal to anyone. She wanted to tell Mrs Clarke because she was a really nice woman but she didn't want to be the bearer of news that would break up what appeared to be a perfect family. She pondered how willing Mr Clarke was to sacrifice church, his wife, and their kids to satisfy his animalistic, lust-filled cravings for vagina. Was it because he no longer found his wife attractive, as she was no longer the petite damsel he met back in her twenties? This thought highly infuriated Velma, as the sixty-two-year-old deacon was no lightweight himself, making the average sumo wrestler look like a rubber toy as his belly mushroomed over his belt. Velma always found it disturbing how men made their women's lives a living hell, complaining about how their women looked while never considering their own appearance. It was as though men expected women to remain unblemished dolls despite giving birth to children and having to wear multiple hats to raise them.

Every Sunday, Velma would watch as Mr Clarke, filled with the Holy Spirit, would speak in tongues, pray for the weak, heal the sick, and prophesy. Disgusted, she would think about how Candy was paid more than her weekly wage in five minutes. She needed to find another job quickly.

All men are dogs, she concluded. There was no damn difference between the deacon and Starboy, the player who chose to hurt her and her daughter by spending all his money on whores despite her loyalty to him and her dreams of a family.

CHAPTER ELEVEN

The Struggle

————————◆◆◆————————

Walking through the village one evening, on her way home from college, Susan heard the voice of her neighbour, Latoya Maynard. Knowing that Latoya despised the ground she walked on, Susan quickened her pace in a bid to avoid any confrontation. "Slow down, bitch! You think your mock hair and bleached skin make you special? Your father is still a whore and your mother is a thief!" shouted Latoya.

Hearing her mother being called a thief struck a nerve. Susan felt a need to defend her mother, as Velma was all she had. The quietened demons in her arose. She flung her bag to the ground, revealing her sanitary napkins, bleaching cream and books. "How dare you call my mother a thief? You black idiot!" she screamed as she lunged for Latoya's hair.

Latoya was somewhat of a tomboy and usually had her short hair covered with a bandanna or a hat. Latoya was also bigger and stronger than Susan, as she often sparred with the boys on the block. As Susan's hand grabbed Latoya's hair, she was left holding the bandanna. Latoya wasted no time grabbing Susan's hair and throwing her to the ground. Susan tried to get up but to no avail. Latoya was kicking and stomping Susan in her face as she dragged her across the road.

As Susan was being pummelled like black pepper seeds with a mortar and pestle, one of her buttons became loose, exposing her original blackness. This fired up Latoya even more, as she was hell-bent on totally humiliating Susan. Latoya reached down and tore the shirt completely open, revealing Susan's black torso. Latoya wanted to draw blood, and that she did. Blood flowed from Susan's brown face and her black torso. Blood also soiled her pants as it was her time of month.

The entire village watched. The young and the old—everyone was trying to get the best vantage point to record the fight on their mobile phones. Dirty, perverse men, instead of being called to action as responsible adults to preserve the peace, were only too eager to see a piece of exposed flesh—the inner thigh, the ass, or breasts. "Yes, Yes!" they shouted as they were granted their reward. Even Benjamin kept positioning himself close to the combatants, as though he was the official referee for the fight. No one lifted a finger as Latoya continued her savagery. Latoya was only stopped when Velma, with the power of one thousand horses, blindsided Latoya with a kick to her face which knocked Latoya to the ground, rendering her senseless.

Yvette, who was watching all along, ran into her house cursing and came back out with a sword but was quickly restrained by her younger son. "You kicked my daughter in her face? Do you think that she is a dog? I am going to chop you up!" screamed Latoya's mother.

Velma heard the shouting but totally ignored it as she was concerned only about Susan, who was crying uncontrollably. Velma picked up Susan's bag and its contents and helped her to stand. Their house was only ten feet away but the mortifying walk of shame felt like a mile.

Velma didn't have any antiseptic cream or gauze, so she got a clean cloth with a bowl of water and used them to clean Susan's wounds.

"Why did she call you a thief, Mom?" cried Susan.

Since Velma did not know what else Susan had heard, she decided to tell her the truth about being fired from work for stealing the bleaching cream. "Mom, oh God, mom, I'm so sorry! I feel like such a fool," Susan sobbed.

As Velma wrung the cloth, the water became saturated with blood. Susan stared at her reflection in the bloodied water and wondered how massa was allowed to make blackness ugly. Her eyes were now opened and she saw who she was, not through her complexion but through the blood that ran through her veins.

She swore within her heart not to let her self-worth be measured by looks, popularity, or education. She looked at her mother and saw a queen, with uninterrupted majestic blackness. She then looked at herself, shook her head, and smiled. That night, she threw away the remaining bleaching cream and hair relaxer.

Over the next couple of months, Susan matured drastically, becoming more comfortable in her skin as it gradually returned to its original hue. She allowed her natural hair to grow, only cutting the relaxed ends. The stares and jeers no longer penetrated her core. Instead she pitied the people who incessantly insulted her. It seemed as though the darker she became, the stronger she was and the more resolve she had. She asked herself, *How can we as blacks progress while hating the skin we live in? We have continued from where massa stopped. The white man whipped, robbed, and killed us and now we do the same to ourselves. Every week in the news or on social media there is a story about a black man killed by his own.* Susan shuddered to think what her forefathers would think if they were alive to witness black people still in bondage. *Maybe the statue of Bussa, erected on the highway with its broken chains and clenched fists, would be better depicted with the chains fully intact. Maybe, instead of posing in the sun daily with his exposed torso, Bussa should return to the plantation.*

As she thought about the bravery of her ancestors who chose to die in the fight for equality, she imagined what kind of slave she would have been. Would she have fought or willingly boarded the boat? As she thought about her answer, a blackbird caught her attention. She watched as the oil on its black feathers caused the white light to separate into a full spectrum of colours, such iridescent beauty. The blackbird walked with purpose and held its head high and in that moment she wished that black people would view themselves in the same way she viewed that blackbird. However, blackness in everyday language was used to represent ugliness, devastation, and negativity, conveyed in words such as black magic, black market and blackmail. As a result, black people rarely saw the beauty and greatness in themselves.

This was compounded as true black history wasn't being taught in schools. The lessons on black history always seemed diluted so as not to offend the powers that be. Emphasis should be placed on promoting black history every day to combat the deliberate attempt to erase historical evidence showcasing the greatness of black people. Instead of being restricted to one month a year during black history month.

Susan wanted to help her mother and was able to find a part-time job working as a library assistant at the college, where she was paid a weekly stipend. This was perfect, as Susan loved to read and was like a cat surrounded by milk. She seized every opportunity to read new books. One day while Susan was reshelving books, she came across some very interesting books which opened her eyes.

She thought it very ironic that blacks depended on white archaeologists and white historians to educate them about Africa when it was the African engineers who built the first great empires in Africa with unparalleled precision using their sophisticated tools. African merchants also conducted their trade with mathematical instruments which would become the envy of future civilizations. Now, these African artefacts were locked away in white-owned museums for a privileged few to view.

Few see the contributions of blacks in building, mathematics, technology, and medicine. Most people don't know that blacks invented touch-tone phones, caller ID, fibre optic cable, closed-circuit television, two-way microphones, pacemakers, stoplights, and the list goes on. It would be remiss of us to think that the nearly thirteen million slaves shipped off during the slave trade were only used for their brute strength and not also for their advanced knowledge.

To this day the black man is mainly portrayed as violent and vengeful in the media. Violence should never be promoted but the black man has every right to be angry due to his race constantly being demonised and exploited. The Jews and the Native Indians are continually being compensated for atrocities committed against them. However, the black race, a people who suffered for more than four hundred years, have not been recompensed.

It seems like no one gives a shit about the suffering of blacks. For instance, was there a worldwide outcry when Belgian King Leopold II killed over ten million black people, wiping out over half the population of Congo? Hell no! Did Rwanda receive any support from Western governments for the genocide where approximately seventy percent of the Tutsi population was killed only two decades ago? Hell no!

Why was this so? Susan wanted to find answers but as she kept looking, more questions were presented. *Why is the black message stifled? What is the black message? Do blacks have a unified voice? Or do blacks find comfort in things which help to ease the pain while ignoring the truth? How do we contribute to our demise as a people?* Susan's mind was filled with questions.

Over time, the additional income allowed them to make improvements to the house. They replaced the termite-infested wood and added three additional rooms. Finally, they each had their own bedroom and a shared bathroom. There was nothing like having indoor plumbing, which was the norm for most people but a luxury for them.

The first day that Susan took a bath indoors, she felt as though she was under a cascading stream of almond milk. She spent hours in the shower and was late for classes but did not care. There was still only one bed and Susan opted for her mom to keep it. Susan stuffed a couple of her old T-shirts with cloth to make a temporary mattress which she positioned in the corner of her room. The space was so small that her arm span was approximately equal to the width of her room, but it felt huge to her. This extra room was a welcome addition, as Susan was now grown and the ladies needed more space. The expansion was a catalyst for Susan's and Velma's progression.

Velma continued to work for Mr Clarke and his wife and she was also able to secure a job maintaining the church and its premises. Even with the extra income it was hard to pay all their bills and save for house improvements, but Velma persevered.

As her house started to take shape and increase in size, so did the envy within the village. The anguish in her neighbours' faces made it seem like they felt the striking of every nail in their bones as the nails were being hammered into the wood to build her house.

It seemed like black people genuinely didn't like to see each other progressing at any level. Susan saw that although the white man had everything, the black man would still be supportive of him obtaining more. It was as if the blacks had an unspoken understanding that whites deserved wealth and the black man deserved poverty.

CHAPTER TWELVE

The Sacrifice

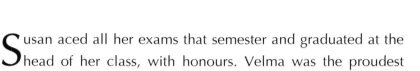

Susan aced all her exams that semester and graduated at the head of her class, with honours. Velma was the proudest mother at the graduation ceremony. She never formally advanced her academics. However, staying up all those late nights as Susan read aloud while revising impacted Velma positively.

Velma was ecstatic and cried tears of joy for Susan as Susan received her degree. That piece of paper didn't just represent Susan's qualifications. It was symbolic of her journey both past and present, her sacrifice, her struggle, and her maturity. As Velma watched Susan make her way off the platform to rejoin her graduating class, Velma's thoughts briefly flashed back to a situation which occurred at the supermarket where Gary, a white, distant relative of Mr Williams, was trained by senior staff members who prepared him for a senior-level management position. Gary was twenty-two years old. He had dropped out of school at age sixteen and had absolutely no qualifications for the job. However, he was given the post only after a few weeks of training and placed in charge of the same persons who trained him. The staff bickered with hushed tones, especially those with experience and university qualifications who thought that they were in line for promotion only to be disappointed. No one even dared to raise their concerns with Mr Williams for fear of being fired. Velma realised that she pushed Susan really hard to get her degree. However, this was only a stepping stone, as there was definitely no guarantee of job security as an employee.

As the weeks passed, Susan filled out several applications and eagerly awaited responses. Every day she would rush to the door to greet the postman, who without fail brought a bill of some kind. She was an active woman and liked being busy, accustomed to juggling several activities, so this so-called vacation period was somewhat disconcerting.

One day, as she was lying on the floor and staring at the ceiling, she was hot and paralysed with boredom. She heard a familiar knock. It was the postman. She had, however, by this time tamed her anxiety, so as not to be repeatedly disappointed. The postman did not see or hear her, so he forced the letters through a space in the door. Her head followed the sound as the envelopes hit the floor. These envelopes looked different to the ones which she was accustomed to. Her heart raced as she scrambled on all fours towards the door like an excited puppy rushing to greet its owner.

These letters were addressed to her. Her palms got wet with anticipation while opening the first letter. As she read it, her posture changed, her shoulders dropped, and her head bowed to the ground. Trying to remain optimistic, she crossed her fingers while reaching for the second letter. She slowly opened it, as if expecting a surprise. She screamed at the top of her lungs when she saw these six words: "We are pleased to inform you..."

She dropped the letter and started skipping around the house with her imaginary rope until she became breathless and was forced to regain her composure. She then squared her shoulders and asserted her posture. She held the letter in her outstretched hands like a scroll and read it aloud.

Velma was about to open the door when she heard a strange voice on the inside. She could not believe it was Susan, who was so in character that she didn't even recognize that Velma had entered. At the end of Susan's imaginary proclamation, she saw her mother's puzzled face and she screamed, "I got the job, Mom!" Susan was offered a position as a teller for a commercial bank. Velma thanked the Lord, as she knew that it was the job Susan really wanted.

The next day was Saturday and Velma was off from work so the ladies decided to go shopping, as Susan didn't have any appropriate outfits to wear. This was going to be an experience for them since it was the first time they had ever gone shopping together. Their previous individual visits to the city were focussed on Susan shopping for school supplies and Velma for work. However, this time was going to be different. The mother and daughter duo were on a mission as they got ready that morning and headed toward the city.

While they were on the bus it came to a halt as major road works were being conducted. This road leading to the city had needed fixing for years. Locals had complained to no avail. However, the government decided to finally fix the stretch of highway because white royalty was going to be visiting the island in a couple of weeks and would be using that road to commute.

Susan, as she sat gazing aimlessly through the window, saw black men working feverishly to complete the road in time. She thought of the times when black dignitaries from African nations visited the island. However, there was never any urgency to fix the highway before their visit. Susan asked herself, *Why would the money collected from taxes not be used for the taxpayers' benefit but be used to impress the white royals?*

The bus was allowed to continue and they finally reached the city. Susan was extremely observant, as she wanted to understand the dynamics of city life to prepare herself mentally for the new job. The city was fast-paced, industrious, busy, and congested. The air was heavy, with its blanket of smog created by toxic emissions of vehicular traffic. Drivers were visibly frustrated and concerned as they narrowly avoided injuring carefree pedestrians who ignored stoplights and darted between cars.

The city was divided by how the businesses were grouped and not by borders. The commercial banks, insurance companies, large department stores, and major restaurants occupied the main streets. The secondary streets were lined with smaller stores, which were less extravagant in their appearance. The back streets, however, were littered with hawkers, hustlers, and numerous rum shops. Where were the local whites? Susan saw white tourists but it seemed like the local whites hardly conducted their business in the city and definitely not in the back streets.

The streets were crowded with men aimlessly congregating by the corners. They constantly petitioned and heckled every woman that passed as though the women were brainless body parts on an assembly line, being inspected and either accepted or rejected according to the specifications of the inspector.

"Darkie, I like how your camel toe looks in those jeans!" one shouted while grabbing his crotch. Velma, having more experience, squeezed Susan's hand to stop her from responding. Susan noticed that there were a lot of women: old and young women, pregnant women, women balancing toddlers on their hips while holding bags without any assistance, women shopping, and women working.

They chose to peruse one of the most popular department stores on the main street since they usually frequented the other stores on the back streets. It was awesome, with fancy lighting fixtures, big beautiful tiles, spacious aisles, nicely dressed Caucasian mannequins, soft background music, and air conditioned comfort.

"Can I help you?" asked an employee as she stared at the ladies from head to toe with a look of disdain. As Velma was about to respond, she was abruptly interrupted by the employee who said, "It's quite ok," and hurriedly went to the assistance of a more astute customer.

"Wow, Mom!" Susan said as she shook her head in disbelief at the level of unprofessionalism they had just experienced.

"Don't worry, love." Velma took one of the shoes off the stand to see the price. Velma's eyes rolled back in her head. She felt faint and almost dropped the shoe, but quickly recovered and said, "Babes, it's time to leave." Velma genuinely felt bad, as she had decided to delay her bill payments and use her weekly wages to shop for Susan. She wanted the best for her daughter but the best would require a lot more money. Her modesty in apparel was always governed by the limitations of her budget and her lack of exposure but this was a tough pill to swallow as she reflected on the price of the pair of shoes, which was twice her wages.

They briskly made their way through the door and down the alley to Velma's familiar spot. It was dark, stuffy, and hot, with hardly any room to manoeuvre. However, they were able to get a couple of outfits for Susan. The ladies had every intention of spending more time in the city, but the episode at the department store knocked the wind out of their sails.

A week had passed since they went shopping. It was now Monday morning and Susan arose full of excitement, ready for her first day at work. Susan arrived an hour early and sat in the lobby with Judy, the security guard, who amused her to help calm her nerves. The distant, click-clacking sound of heels striking the tiles reverberated throughout the empty hallway. "That's Mrs Jackson coming," Judy said without looking up.

"Who is Mrs Jackson?" asked Susan.

"Oh, she's the branch manager," whispered Judy as the sound of the heels got louder. "I can't stand that lying bitch," she continued.

"Good morning, Mrs Jackson. You look lovely today as usual," said Judy while smiling from ear to ear with a sparkle in her eyes.

"Good morning, ladies. Thank you, Judy. You say the sweetest things."

"Good morning," Susan said nervously.

"Good morning. Susan Lynch, correct?" asked Mrs Jackson.

"Yes ma'am," croaked Susan.

"Come with me," said Mrs Jackson as she led the way.

As Susan followed, she recalled what Judy said. This was her first day and Judy was already attempting to sow seeds of distrust in Susan's mind regarding Mrs Jackson. Susan decided not to prejudice her opinion of Mrs Jackson until she got to know her. She also decided to keep her guard up around Judy based on how quickly she was able to curse and bless with the same tongue.

Susan was given a tour of the office. While being introduced to the staff, she realized that the tellers were mostly young, slender, light-skinned women. However, the older, darker ladies usually held positions in the back office.

Directly after her tour, training commenced. She caught on well and was soon doing basic tasks without supervision. Over the next couple of weeks, Susan became very proficient and was showing a noticeable level of attention to detail. She was always punctual and extremely helpful. Her probationary period was going very well.

The bank was a very active one, servicing hundreds of customers daily. Susan, being a teller, was able to draw several conclusions from observation and customers' account information, to which she was privy. She never shared this information but she pondered to herself about her observations.

She saw the disparity of wealth amongst the blacks and the whites. Most of the whites were wealthy business owners having millions or access to millions. They were the bank's premium wealth customers. Their children were usually employed by the family business at very young ages and they also kept money in their community longer by supporting each other.

They were owners of very large tangible assets which could be used to obtain mortgages, loans, overdrafts, and other banking facilities with relative ease. The land which whites inherited from the days of slavery or bought at extremely cheap rates would be used as collateral to help them acquire and develop businesses while exploiting blacks with menial pay, thereby continuing the cycle of white business owners and black labourers.

Susan also noticed that some blacks were very wealthy and owned their own businesses. However, this was the exception, as blacks were usually employees living paycheque to paycheque. Very few blacks owned businesses and when they did, they were serviced with high debt as opposed to capital and provided low income. She saw a high percentage of foreclosures and repossessions of black-owned properties and assets while other blacks were even poorer, with no cash on their accounts.

Susan recalled how her mother bellowed in her ears as a young child to go to school to learn and get a good job. She saw how this traditional mindset, even though well-meaning in its motivation, supported the lack of entrepreneurial thinking amongst blacks. Traditional thinking taught the black man how to be an employee while entrepreneurial exposure taught the white man how to own his own business. Blacks were taught to "get a good job." However, whites were taught to "own businesses" which created the jobs. This dynamic flowed naturally in a society where blacks were historically labourers and whites were labour owners. Survival of the blacks depended on how diligently and productively they laboured. Survival of the whites depended on how well their businesses performed. It all made sense to Susan now as she was in an institution where she could see the real-life by-products of both paths.

Whites, on the backs of black slaves, were given an unfair advantage which caused whites to prosper for generations. Susan wondered, *How do you truly recompense black people who suffered so harshly and continue to suffer?* Slaves were ripped from their homes and lives, whipped unmercifully, raped, and killed while working on plantation land to fatten massa's pockets. These pockets bursting with cash allowed massa to continue his expansion by placing a significant economic divide between the two races. This allowed the white man to continue conquering at the top of the pyramid as the merchant, while the black man continued struggling at the bottom of the pyramid as the consumer.

The white man had been in a place of dominance for so long due to his commanding wealth that it almost seemed preposterous to think of a poor white man on the island. Why would it be unthinkable to see a homeless white-skinned, blue-eyed, blonde lying in the city gutter? Why would it be unthinkable to see a white person sweeping the city streets? Or living in one of the poor back streets? It was, however, normal to see black homeless men and women. It was normal to see black janitors and maids. It was normal to see black men and women at the bottom of the barrel.

The stark differences between blacks and whites relating to wealth and poverty were just heartbreaking. Susan called to mind that everywhere she looked, whether in the countryside or the city, there were reminders.

Only blacks could be seen lining up religiously every morning waiting for assistance from one of the Salvation Army's eleven branches across the island. Whites were never to be found in a line waiting for any kind of charitable assistance.

Only blacks were found walking to their destinations or waiting at bus stops for the bus. Susan never saw whites taking public transportation or walking through sun or rain to various locations.

Only blacks lived in the impoverished government units. Whites were never found in any of the poverty-stricken ghetto areas. No whites lived in deplorable conditions like where Velma and Susan lived. Barbados was such a small island, with a level of segregation so extremely stark.

Susan could not understand what it was about black skin on this small island that made it acceptable for blacks to live like less than second class citizens and nearly riot if a similar plight was even suggested for the white man. *Is it that we secretly think that white skin genuinely cannot bear to toil and grind in the harsh elements without demise?*

As Susan worked, she continued to ponder on this divide. Was it because whites were born with golden spoons in their mouths? Maybe! Was it because whites had an unfair advantage in the form of free land, free labour, and freedom to do as they pleased? Who wouldn't be rich if they had four hundred years of free labour and resources?

Susan thought to herself that what needed to happen to right this wrong would be somewhat of fantasy but nothing less would even begin to address the poverty-stricken plight of the black man. She had heard people speak of reparations before but reparations alone would not rectify the problem. She knew that reparation was making amends for the wrong done by paying money to or otherwise helping those who had been wronged. So reparation as a solution would be like a drop of water in the sea. Some might say that something was better than nothing. However, reparations alone could never begin to right the wrongs if the aim wasn't to level the playing field.

Susan paused to think of reparations as being like someone nearly beating you to death, placing you in a hole, stealing your ladder to climb to a place where food and treasure were stored. They then ate all of the food, took all of the treasure and then decided to give you back a ladder which was now not only shorter but also out of reach. Should you be thankful? Of what purpose is the ladder to you now that the food is gone and the treasure stolen?

The only fair thing to do would be to divide the spoils equally at every level. Whatever the whites of today were able to obtain from their forefathers, who rode on the backs of slaves, should be shared equally amongst whites and blacks.

All that the white man had should be co-owned—his land, his property, and his businesses—by a well-thought-out government strategy which benefitted both blacks and whites by equally distributing wealth and power. This strategy would be unlike reckless initiatives of property and business acquisition tried unsuccessfully in the past by some African nations.

If whites continued to solely prosper from the atrocities that were committed during slavery, what real differences can be expected? The whites' wealth shouldn't just continue to benefit them and their offspring. It should also benefit the blacks and their offspring as well, since the black man's forefathers contributed majorly to the white man's wealth. The black man should be able to gain more than by just being an employee and should be rewarded by also having a commanding stake in the businesses.

Black people should be joint owners on boards, able to make decisions. There should be such a levelling of the playing field that the societal norms would change drastically. It would be normal for whites to work for blacks and for whites to work in the public sector. It would also be normal for blacks to own large conglomerates and established enterprises.

The norm would be for both whites and blacks to attend public primary, secondary, and tertiary schools and for more blacks to attend private schools. Susan thought of her days at school and how she hardly saw any white students in class. Rarely were whites ever to be found at any of the primary public schools, and only a few whites attended the top secondary public schools. Whites were hardly seen at the local community college or the local university due to either being drafted into the family enterprise where they learnt pivotal business skills or studying at prestigious colleges and universities overseas, funded by their parents. In hindsight, Susan understood that the whites paid to keep their children separated, through private schooling, in their early developmental years.

Whites patronising black-owned businesses should be as normal as blacks patronising white-owned businesses. The whites tended to patronise and support their own businesses and events. They hardly supported the local black-owned businesses. For many years hawkers would line the streets and fill the local markets, especially on Saturdays, to sell their fruit, vegetables, locally made condiments, and other provisions. Whites, for the most part, scarcely ventured to these markets to shop. However, in more recent years whites started markets on their own properties and on Saturdays and Sundays the overwhelming support by both blacks and whites for the initiative could be seen.

It would be normal for both white-owned and black-owned businesses to have a fair chance at success or failure. Susan noted that white businesses did better because they had the capital to invest and the support from other whites to keep the businesses' doors open. Black businesses, however, without capital or support, struggled to be successful and had almost no chance of ever being at the top.

Black night clubs in Barbados had opened and closed throughout the years but the one nightclub that had remained open through the test of time was ironically a white-owned club. Many blacks owned hardware stores and mini-marts but very few of them reached the level of mega stores or supermarkets. Susan remembered one of the earlier black-owned supermarkets on its way to the top abruptly saw its end, leaving at the time only white-owned supermarkets.

Susan knew that the unlevel playing field of wealth caused by the black man's exploitation through slavery was responsible in part for the poorer neighbourhoods having higher levels of crime and young women having many children, usually with hardly any income to support them, leaving them and their children vulnerable.

Susan thought about what Velma told her about Candy, the young prostitute. The hustle was serious for her. She would end up entertaining all types of unfavourable characters, which exposed her child to prostitution, drugs, and guns at an early age. It is very difficult for young impressionable minds to stay focussed with a lot of them engaging in criminal activities. More often than not they become delinquent, ending up on the wrong side of the law with a criminal record, making it difficult for them to find gainful employment.

Everyone likes progression and that was what money afforded blacks who were blessed with the opportunity to amass money and in some cases wealth, allowing them to rise above their dismal situation and usually move out of the communities in which they grew up. They pay top dollar for a piece of the rock and build massive structures, purchasing the majority of their building materials from white-owned suppliers. They buy expensive cars from one of the several white-owned distributors since there are no black-owned new car dealers on the island.

Susan's experience at the bank was an interesting one, to say the least. Every day she met varying personalities with differing degrees of temperament. She was never officially trained in customer relations; however, she was well read and had an appreciation for people. This, coupled with Velma's teachings, played a vital role in dealing with some of the most wretched individuals. Susan clearly possessed a very enviable quality, being able to quell the most outrageous arguments, not only as it related to customers but internally with her peers. Mrs Jackson was extremely happy to have Susan on board and regularly praised her efforts.

One day Mrs Jackson called Susan into her office and asked her to close the door. "Have a seat, Susan," said Mrs Jackson. "I have been watching you for a while and would like to recommend you for a temporary position in private banking, as one of the ladies will be going on maternity leave." Susan was rendered speechless as she stood there with her mouth slightly open just enough for her spirit to exit and cartwheel around the office.

"Susan, Susan," Mrs Jackson called while looking into Susan's eyes as though looking through the window of an empty house.

Susan's spirit hurriedly took back up residence. "Hi Mrs Jackson, thank you so much," Susan said as Mrs Jackson opened the door for her to exit. *She is a lying bitch,* Judy's voice echoed in her head, causing Susan to stop in her tracks.

"Is everything ok, Susan?" asked Mrs Jackson as Susan placed her hand to her temple as though in deep thought.

"Sorry, yes ma'am," she said as she returned to her station.

Susan was very careful throughout the day not to wear her excitement on her sleeve, as she saw the inquisitive stares of her colleagues. She knew it was news that she had to keep to herself until it was official. She was also still very new to the bank and expected a significant fallout because of the offer she was given.

That evening, Susan could not wait to leave work, as it was Velma's birthday and she wanted to buy her mother a gift and share the exciting news. As the workday drew to a close, Susan reconciled her cash and logged out of her terminal. "Good evening, folks; have a nice evening and see you tomorrow," she said as usual. However, this evening was different, as the deafening silence was the loudest response she had ever gotten. It was amazing how envy was starting to take shape because of a closed office door.

As Susan made her way through the door and down the hall, she saw Judy beckoning to her in the distance. As she got closer Judy said, "I heard that you met with lying Jackson and you may be in for a raise."

Susan was amazed at the lightning speed with which gossip travelled. "I met with Mrs Jackson but I don't know about any raise. Anyhow, it's my mother's birthday and I have to go," said Susan as she looked at the clock and hurried off.

As Susan briskly walked through the city, she passed the same guys on the same corner. These guys seemed to be anchored there religiously, as she saw them on her way to and from work every day. Things were hard but these black men seemed content with swinging dicks instead of building bricks. These guys showed absolutely no ambition. They possessed the eyes of fatherless souls, deep and dark. Their taut facial muscles were programmed to intimidate. Their shirtless backs exposed their newfound black canvas, saturated with ink. Their battle scars were worn as badges of honour. Some of them wore shoes, while others showcased hardened, crusty soles resembling the pavement. Their pants were worn deliberately low to showcase boxers and butt cracks. What a hybrid of a man! Externally towering, strong and masculine yet internally he was small, weak and feminine. Always angry at the world, always warring with others, while the battle evidently continued within them.

Susan was immune by now to the numerous catcalls she would receive when she passed the block. She could not, however, understand how the same men could aimlessly gather the same place, doing the same thing every day. Maybe this block culture provided a sense of purpose and a chance to feel appreciated by brethren. Just maybe belonging to a crew could be the model adopted for building community spirit.

However, there was one fundamental issue with embracing the block life for Susan. Everyone seemed to be followers, with nobody able to stop the other from going astray. They usually fought with each other. *Where is the sense of community? There is nothing wrong with recreation but it can't be for the entire day. Black men are rolling spliffs and posing, standing idly by while white men are going to the moon and back, if only figuratively speaking. How are we progressing? How do we expect to catch up when our young black men lack vision and are blinded and paralyzed?*

"Darkie, darkie!" one said as he tried feverishly to keep up with Susan and interrupted her thoughts.

"Excuse me! What did you call me?" asked Susan as she stopped abruptly, nearly causing him to run into her.

The guy was going to quickly rejoin his gang when he saw the look on Susan's face. Susan would normally be full of smiles but she felt angered that after so many months of the same routine they never even asked her for her name but kept addressing her by her complexion.

"Darkie!" the guy said.

"Well, that is not my name. My name is Susan; what is yours?" Susan asked angrily.

"All my niggas call me Killa," he said while signalling to his crew.

"Killa? I mean, really?! What is your real name?" Susan asked.

"Jaden," said Jaden.

"With a beautiful name like Jaden, why would you want to call yourself 'Killa?'" Susan asked. "The average black man on the block is already being stereotyped as the bareback hooligan who is always planning to rob and kill," she continued.

"I don't care about what people think. Nobody cares about the ghetto youth. That is why I have to look out for myself and my son," said Jaden as he raised his voice.

Susan had obviously struck a nerve. Jaden, who only minutes before was trying to get into her panties, was now on the warpath as his eyes instantly became red as though ablaze.

"The system is corrupt. The politicians, judges and police—every blasted one of them—are wicked sons of bitches. The law favours the white and the rich. They blatantly commit crimes and don't spend a day behind bars," Jaden continued. "Only the other day a white man with a yacht carrying over half a million dollars in drugs was intercepted by police. He was released scot-free! The same police locked up one of my boys for a five dollar spliff. He will be behind bars for at least three months. For years black men overseas were locked up for selling herb on the streets and now white men are legally selling herb on shelves. Do you see the injustice? Who will tell those black men sorry?" Jaden said.

Susan shook her head as she also recalled reading that a container was found with drugs and guns and the case was thrown out. Again, another white man who had power and influence never received a day in jail. However, an innocent black man was arrested at the airport and escorted by five police officers for an empty container that they accused him of stealing, which he had absolutely no knowledge of.

"That is why I do whatever, whenever, and would kill anyone who gets in my way," said Jaden while forming his fingers to resemble a gun.

"Kill! Oh my God, seriously?! Do you see white men killing and shooting each other in Barbados? Black men are killing black men and then spending their lives behind bars. Can't you see what is going on, Jaden? There are already over fifty murders for the year, all young black men taken out of the world in their prime. The dead ones are not the only victims. Their mothers are left to grieve, their children are left to suffer, and their entire communities are void of their contribution," replied Susan. "Are you not afraid of prison?" she added.

"Afraid of prison?! Prison is no harder than out here and at least there, I will be fed!" Jaden said with a shrug.

"But Jaden, you have a son, and if you go to prison or die you will be leaving him without a father," said Susan.

"Listen girl, life is rough out here and we all have to die. That is why I am already showing my son the ropes," said Jaden as he walked away from her to chase another skirt.

Susan thought of Jaden's son and how such an innocent life would be affected by his father's reality. He would be judged by the same measuring rod as others who had better opportunities to excel.

Susan understood from the five minutes that she spoke to Jaden why so many black men were behind bars. She wished she had more time to talk to him but time was getting away and Susan was on a mission. She was heading to the department store where the shoes that nearly took her mother's life were.

Upon entering, Susan headed directly for the shoe section. "Good evening, how may I help?" It was the same obnoxious sales lady from before. This time she was all smiles while rubbing her hands together as though creaming them.

"Do you have size eight in this style?" Susan asked.

"We certainly do, ma'am. Please have a seat while I fetch them for you," said the sales lady as she scurried off. Before Susan could be properly seated, the lady was back. "You are in luck, dear. These are the last pair of size eights. Would you like to try them?" said the sales lady.

"No thank you. Can I get them wrapped, please? They are for my mom's birthday," Susan said while walking toward the cashier.

"Certainly," said the sales lady.

Susan ventured up to the next floor and chose a cell phone for herself. She reached the cashier just ahead of a white lady and was about to pay when the cashier called the white lady forward. "But I was here first!" said Susan.

"Please wait your turn, ma'am," the cashier replied as the white lady squeezed between Susan and the counter to get in front. Susan was dumbfounded. "Next customer," the cashier said.

"You're telling me that you honestly didn't see me here first when you called her from behind me?!" an irate Susan said as she paid her money.

"Don't you know who that was?! That was Mrs Corbin," said the cashier as she beckoned the next customer.

CHAPTER THIRTEEN

A Daughter's Wish

———————◆———————

L ater that evening as Susan was walking towards her house, Starboy was driving away. As she turned the knob and entered, she saw a startled Velma, partially naked in only her panties, hurriedly picking up her clothing from off the ground. Susan was never able to come to grips with her emotions as they related to Starboy.

She knew about bucks and how they did not have any loyalty to any woman or family. However, this was no longer something she read in a book; this was personal for Susan. This was about her not having a father she could call Dad, a father with whom she could share her feelings. She didn't have that male figure in her life to keep her safe and secure.

She didn't have an example to follow, since he abandoned her from birth and never showed her any affection. However, this dirty man void of decency was allowed to effortlessly disrespect her mother, who was her only source of strength over the years. She didn't want to hate him, but the feelings of resentment were high. Susan decided to ignore her feelings once again and not confront her mother, because it was her fortieth birthday and she wanted her to be happy. "Mom, come here please. I have a surprise for you."

Velma, still embarrassed, approached timidly. Susan gave her mom the box and told her to open it. Velma in all her years had never received a gift for her birthday and started to cry as she feebly tried to remove the wrapping paper. It wouldn't have made a difference what the gift was; she was just overwhelmed with emotions. However, when she saw that her daughter had bought her the shoes that they saw but couldn't afford when shopping together, she rejoiced as though she had won the lottery.

Weeks passed, and Susan was given the job in private banking. The few friends she thought she had stopped speaking to her and once again, Susan was isolated. The ladies in the new department also appeared cold towards her, as though they felt threatened. Susan had not too long ago started at the bank and was already being earmarked for promotion.

One day, as she was sitting at her desk, a shadow darkened the document she was reading. As she slowly looked up she saw Mrs Knight, the Human Resources Manager, standing above her. Mrs Knight was a slender, light-skinned lady with short wavy hair and green eyes that she inherited from her white grandmother. She was always sure to mention the white side of her family with a sense of pride to everyone who would lend her an ear. However, she hardly spoke about the black side of her family, as though she was ashamed of their very existence. Mrs Knight was extremely vocal and intimidating and inspected Susan from head to toe as she stood over her. "Please don't get too comfortable as this position is only temporary and, in my opinion, I don't think that you are the best fit for the bank's premium customers," she said and left without waiting for a response.

Susan loved her job and stayed clear of conflict. Mrs Knight's seniority was also a bit intimidating and Susan struggled with mentioning her concerns to Mrs Jackson. After a while of not being able to concentrate, she decided to go to Mrs Jackson. Mrs Jackson, on the phone, motioned for Susan to have a seat. "Hi Susan, how can I help you today?" Mrs Jackson said as soon as she hung up.

"Well, Mrs Knight just told me that I wasn't the right fit," Susan said cautiously, not fully knowing how Mrs Jackson would genuinely deal with it.

"Oh Lord, no! Tell me she didn't. I fought against all odds for that opportunity for you. My decision was not superficial but based on your work ethic. I will deal with it," Mrs Jackson said as she stood up.

Susan looked deep into Mrs Jackson's eyes, as though trying to connect with her soul. As Susan got up to leave the office, she felt comforted that Mrs Jackson was telling her the truth. Susan was normally a diligent worker but decided to work even harder. She wanted to make Mrs Jackson proud for believing in her.

One day as she was about to leave for the day, she was surprised to hear the guard opening the door to allow a customer in, as the official banking hours were over. "Good evening," she heard. A tall, handsome white man in his mid-thirties stood there, smiling as he watched her. It was Mr Corbin, one of the bank's premium customers. He was very wealthy and highly admired by most of the women. Today he was casually dressed in his customary khaki-coloured cargo pants, a white polo shirt and tan-coloured deck shoes. Mr Corbin's attire always fascinated Susan, as he always seemed so confident, never having to dress to impress like the black men who didn't have half of his wealth. "I will be travelling and wanted to give you this document before I leave tomorrow," he said.

For the first time, Susan felt a difference, as a million butterflies were aimlessly flying around in her stomach. She watched his big blue eyes. They were like beams which lit up the room. His hair was sandy brown with streaks of blonde and his skin was smooth and tanned.

Susan had absolutely no experience with men and her innocence shone through. Mr Corbin smiled as he gave her his card and held her hand for what seemed like an eternity. His touch was manly and warm. Susan, still awestruck, watched as he exited the room. She was about to leave but sat for a while to catch her breath. As she sat there she decided to add his contact information to her phone.

She was excited but still didn't fully understand why. *Should I call him now or should I wait? Should I call him, or should I message him? I should probably message him ...but what do I say?* Susan tied herself in a mental knot that evening. She finally pulled herself from behind her desk, as she had spent a while daydreaming.

That night, Susan picked up her phone, determined to message Mr Corbin, but could not muster the courage. The next day, however, she was really distracted and could not concentrate, as the decision to call or not was overwhelming.

She finally decided to message, as he was off the island and that would buy her time just in case she made a fool of herself. "Hi, this is Susan," she typed. The two minutes she waited for him to respond felt like two years, but it was worth the wait. He sent a smiley face and said it was about time, to which she responded with a smile. The two exchanged numerous messages over the next couple of weeks, with Susan trying to remain mindful that Mr Corbin was a busy man.

Mr Corbin played polo as a hobby and Susan was really eager to attend a match, as the bank was a major sponsor. A match was coming up in a few days and Susan tried hard not to bring it up, hoping deep inside that he would invite her. She made up her mind that whether he invited her or not, she would attend to show her support. She spent the next couple of days preparing herself for the big event.

The day came and Susan, along with a few of her colleagues, was allowed to attend. She was totally flabbergasted by how beautifully landscaped the property was, with its lush, massive polo field and commanding club house. The car park was filled to capacity, with a full range of luxury cars and Jeeps. Susan had never seen so many white people gathered in one place before. She found it even more shocking that it was a weekday, around two in the afternoon, when most black people would have been at work.

The sound of horses galloping and the mud exploding as their hooves impacted the ground signalled the start of the game. Watching Mr Corbin as he rode his beast like a white knight, swinging his long wooden mallet, striking the ball with masterful precision while maintaining his balance, was immensely intriguing to Susan. She could not keep her eyes off him.

It was half-time now and no sooner had the players dismounted than young black boys eagerly ran to take the horses to give them water and prepare them for the second half of the game. Susan was filled with nervousness as Mr Corbin approached her direction but all of her preparation was for naught, as he walked right by her, not even acknowledging her presence as he stopped to talk to some people directly behind her. She was crushed.

The end of the break was marked by the young black men, who were just excited to play their part in the event by returning the horses to their riders. Susan could not bear to watch the second half of the game due to her emotional state of mind and decided to leave.

That night she didn't receive any calls or texts as usual, which made her feel even worse.

CHAPTER FOURTEEN

The Narrow Escape

The following day after work, Susan was standing by the bus stop as usual when a blue Jeep with heavily tinted windows pulled up. As the window slowly came down, it revealed Mr Corbin. "Get in," he said. As hurt as Susan was the night before, she jumped in the vehicle without hesitation. She was so excited to see him and decided not to mention yesterday so as not to upset him.

As they drove, he reached over and placed his hand on her inner thigh. Susan's body melted at his touch. Her heart was racing, her vagina was throbbing, and her head felt like it would explode. Susan never told Mr Corbin where she lived and didn't even realize when his Jeep pulled into the yard of an abandoned factory and parked at the back of the compound between some heavy machinery.

He stopped and removed his seatbelt. Then he slowly reached over to remove hers, deliberately allowing his chest to touch her nipple, which was bursting out of her shirt. She smelled his skin as his soft beard touched her face. She felt the warmth of his breath as he exhaled.

He looked into her eyes and groaned as he gently pulled her face towards his. He kissed her lips ever so softly, applying just the right amount of pressure as he did. His hands expertly unbuttoned her shirt and with a snap of a finger her bra was off. He fondled and caressed her breasts with one of his hands while the other hand gradually made its way up her skirt.

Experiencing all of these sensations all at once was overwhelming. She was falling fast. However, she definitely didn't want her first time to be in a vehicle after a long, hot day at work. As she attempted to close her legs to restrict his hands from reaching any farther, his phone rang, displaying a picture of a beautiful white lady in her thirties whom Susan could have sworn she saw before and a boy who was the spitting image of Mr Corbin.

He allowed the phone to ring a couple of times as he tried to compose himself and slow his breathing. He also placed his finger on Susan's mouth before he answered, "Hi honey, I just had to make a stop, but I will be home shortly."

Susan's body had gone cold. "Who was that?" she asked, knowing the answer but fearing the response. "Oh, that is just my wife, no need to worry," he said nonchalantly.

Susan was perplexed. "You are married?! Oh my God!" she exclaimed. She really liked him and was foolishly hopeful, as she fantasized about him day and night. As he tried to touch her exposed breasts again, she pushed his hands away violently and shouted, "Why did you lead me on like this?!"

"Oh relax," he laughed. "I always wanted to try a darkie." A lump of realization forcefully made its way down Susan's throat. She had been used.

Susan tried to fasten her bra, but Mr Corbin wouldn't let her as he kept trying to grope her. This once-gentle man became a ravenous beast as he seemed obsessed with getting his hands up her skirt to remove her panties.

She could not believe this was the same man, as she was now panicking and scared for her life. As she felt the tips of his fingers on her private parts, his phone rang again. He allowed it to ring off as he closed his eyes and sniffed his fingers.

He then gave her a stare as cold as ice and said in the most hideous voice ever, "Get out and if you utter this to anyone, I will kill your black ass." Susan had barely gotten her feet out of the Jeep before he raced out of the factory yard, nearly knocking her to the ground.

Here she was in the dark, in the middle of nowhere, cold and scared as hell. She took off her heels and ran as fast as she could to get out of the factory yard, just in case he returned. She was now walking alongside the road, panting, sweating, and crying. She saw lights approaching her and decided to run into the cane field to hide.

As she hid, she heard the voices of her ancestors—men, women and children—screaming in her head. The very canes seemed to come alive and shadows appeared like bodiless souls. This surreal experience, coupled with the trauma she had just been through, caused Susan to think about all the black slave women who were raped while on the slave ships or in the fields in the presence of their loved ones and discarded like trash. After Susan realized that it was just another motorist, she continued walking through the cane field until she got to the bus stop.

CHAPTER FIFTEEN

Regret

———————— ⚜ ————————

When Susan got home that night she was relieved to see that her mother wasn't there yet. She stripped off her clothes and immediately jumped into the shower. She soaked from head to toe and scrubbed her skin profusely, cleansing herself from the ordeal she had just been through. That night as Susan lay on her bed, she started to blame herself for falling so quickly for Mr Corbin. She wondered if deep down inside, she wanted to be with a white man to give herself some form of social validation or security.

Susan tossed and turned that night, trying her best to fall asleep before her mother reached home. Every time she closed her eyes, she would quickly reopen them, as she felt scared. Finally fatigue got the best of her as she helplessly entered into a deep sleep.

The next couple of weeks were hard, as Susan kept seeing Mr Corbin as he came into the bank to conduct business. He continued to greet her as though nothing had happened. One day as she was making her way down the corridor, she heard his voice as he spoke to security. She quickened her pace but it was a long corridor. He also quickened his pace, as Susan could hear running behind her. "Wait up, Susan," he said as he got closer. The hair on her skin stood up as he got next to her. She felt uneasy and nervous. "You need to lighten up and give me some of that oily meat of yours and stop being so obstinate. I can do a lot for you," he said.

One more word and Susan would have definitely thrown up right there and then. Luckily Mrs Knight met them on her way up the corridor and started with her fake-ass hobnobbing shit. "Good morning Mr Corbin, how are you today?" Susan used this as her opportunity to distance herself.

That day at the bank was hard but got better when she found out that she was chosen to attend a seminar in New York. She was elated but nervous, as she had never travelled in her life. She did not know what to expect and with all of her nervous energy, long before she was ready to travel she packed her suitcase with everything except the sofa for her weeklong trip.

CHAPTER SIXTEEN

Shocking

The day came and it was time for Susan's departure. Velma made sure that Susan had her sweetbread, macaroni pie, and baked chicken in her carryon luggage for the five-hour flight ahead. The two hugged, kissed and cried as though they were never going to see each other again. As Susan boarded the plane she was pleasantly surprised by a white lady saying, "Welcome aboard American Airlines."

Susan was happy that she had a window seat and made herself as comfortable as possible while listening attentively to every word from the flight attendant, who was demonstrating the safety procedures. The engines were loud as they powered up, and the seat beneath her vibrated as this aerodynamic masterpiece, a perfect combination of materials and engineering brilliance, defied all logic by lifting off and parting the clouds. As the pressure rose her ears popped and her jaws dropped as Barbados, her world, was reduced to a tiny rock in minutes surrounded by blue.

Susan was in total amazement as she watched the majestic rays that formed a kaleidoscope of colours and the endless skyscape of clouds of all shapes and sizes drifting without restriction. The experience was liberating and peaceful, causing her to think about God in all his glory. *Why did he create all of this? Is he watching? Does he really have favourites?* Susan drifted off to sleep and was awakened hours later by the pilot announcing that they would be landing soon. As she peered through the window, the sheer vastness of the country below was overwhelming.

As this tonnage approached the runway, she fastened her seatbelt really tight and held on to her seat with both hands. Her stomach felt weak. However, there was nothing to fear, as the landing was even less traumatizing than driving over a pothole back home. The loud sounds of the brakes filled the cabin as the plane came to a halt.

As the plane was being taxied into the terminal, Susan was in awe at the enormity of the airport and the numerous planes that were there. She asked herself, *Why aren't there any black owned airlines or black owned aircraft manufacturers?* She never questioned the technical abilities of the black man to accomplish such a feat, but wondered why he didn't own any of the big manufacturing plants for aircrafts, ships, automobiles, trains, machinery, or weapons. *Our brilliance always seems to be harnessed for others to profit, while we remain consumers.*

When she disembarked she was totally shocked to see white people cleaning bathrooms, collecting garbage, and working as immigration officers. She smiled to herself and thought what a sight it would be to see a white sanitation worker or a white man working in a clerical position at one of the public institutions back home, as Bajan whites very seldom worked for anyone besides themselves.

"Goodnight ma'am," the white taxi driver said as he opened the door for her and placed her bags in the trunk.

"Goodnight sir," Susan replied.

"Wait! Are you from Barbados?" the taxi driver asked as soon as he got in the driver's seat.

"Yes, I am," she replied while positioning herself to see his face in the rear view mirror.

"I am a Bajan too. My family are from St. John," he said in the rawest Bajan accent Susan had ever heard. "Where are you staying?" he asked as Susan took out her mobile phone to show him the hotel's address. "This is a very nice hotel," he said, as he placed the address of the hotel in the GPS. He then turned on his indicator and cautiously merged onto the highway.

There was a loud screeching sound of brakes and a horn fiercely blew as an oncoming motorist narrowly avoided colliding with the taxi. "You blasted nigger! Watch where you are going!" said an irate driver as he gave the taxi driver a middle finger.

Susan was visibly shaken by the near miss, but was at a total loss as to why the other driver would be so mean to her, as she was just a passenger. "Why did he call me a nigger?" she asked while holding her neck.

"Are you ok?" the driver asked.

"My neck is just a bit sore, but I will be ok," she said while still waiting for an answer to her previous question. "I asked why he called me a nigger," she repeated while trying to reconcile her thoughts, as they were scattered throughout her brain, causing total confusion.

"He did not mean you. He meant me," the driver finally said, as he was unsuccessful at avoiding the question a second time.

"He meant you! Aren't you white?" Susan asked in astonishment.

"I am white back home in Barbados; however, I got the shock of my life when I first came to this country and was called a nigger less than an hour after arriving," he said.

"I cannot believe that they consider you black here; to me, you look even whiter than most Bajan whites back home," Susan said while shaking her head.

"Well, if you are shocked you should place yourself in my shoes. I lived in Barbados for over twenty-seven years as a white man and I have lived over here for the past twenty-four years as a black man," the taxi driver said while switching lanes. "This experience has definitely been an eye-opener for me.

"I felt privileged to be one of the chosen few. I felt proud to be considered a white man. I felt a sense of accomplishment for something over which I had absolutely no control. I didn't choose my parents; neither did you choose your parents but we still continue to despise each other on the basis of skin colour— what a superficial criteria!" he continued.

Susan fought back tears as she wondered how different the world would be if racism wasn't allowed to infect and poison the human race. As the tears streamed down her face Susan tried distracting herself by taking in all of the sights. She took as many pictures as possible with her phone of the lights, skyscrapers, and traffic. New York was a melting pot of activity, with its millions of people hurrying to and fro, representing all races, colours and sizes. She was just overwhelmed. After about thirty minutes they arrived at the hotel. Susan paid the driver, took her bags, and headed to the lobby to check in and retire to her room for the night.

The hotel room was just gorgeous. It had nice lighting and was beautifully furnished with a double bed with snow-white linen and super cold air conditioning. She took out her food and messaged Velma while eating it, knowing that her mother would not be able to sleep unless she knew that Susan was in safely. After chatting and eating, Susan stripped her clothing and hurried in the shower, as jet lag was starting to kick in.

CHAPTER SEVENTEEN

The Meeting

———————❧———————

Morning came and Susan had overslept and had to rush to the seminar, which luckily for her was being held in a conference room located in the hotel. As she entered the room, Mrs Knight called her over. "Come sit with me, Susan. We're the only two black people here and we need to stick together." Susan nearly fainted, as she never thought that she would hear these words from Mrs Knight. It seemed as though Mrs Knight was now temporarily identifying with the black race, since she was not able to leverage any preferential treatment from her light complexion, as she would have in Barbados, in this environment where black was not seen as shades of colour but as one race.

Mrs Knight transformed, to the point of convincingly having split personalities. She was super sweet to Susan when being ignored by the whites. However, as soon as the whites interacted with her, traits of her old self started to shine through. She ignored Susan and appeared condescending. Susan wondered if the association with white people made Mrs Knight feel accepted.

On the second day of the seminar, as Susan was in the elevator making her way down to the conference room, the elevator stopped on the fifth floor. A tall, dark, handsome guy in his mid-thirties entered. "Good morning ma'am, how are you today?" he said as he positioned himself and selected his floor.

"Good morning, I am ok, and you?" Susan said reservedly, as her last experience with Mr Corbin left her a bit cautious about being alone with men.

"I am well," he said, with a broad smile. "I guess you're here for the seminar?" As she was about to answer, the elevator stopped and the door opened. A middle-aged white lady who was looking at her phone stepped into the elevator and, on recognising that she was surrounded by blacks, she tried to step off but it was too late.

The look on the white lady's face made the simple elevator ride seem like a rapid, hell-bound plummet. Her nervous grimace carved contours for her sweat to trace as it made its way down her neck and into her blouse. Her veins seemed to rest on top of her flesh as she clenched her bag tighter. The elevator stopped on the next floor and as the door slowly opened, revealing another black face, the white lady seemed as if her fate had been sealed for sure as she closed her eyes and waited for what must have seemed like an eternity to her for the elevator to reach the ground floor. As the door opened, she exhaled loudly as she was released and free to escape her captors.

"Yes, I am here for the seminar. I apologise for my manners," Susan said to the gentleman as they exited the elevator and made their way down the corridor.

"Your accent is nice. Where are you from?" he asked.

"I am from Barbados," Susan replied.

"Oh, Jamaica?" he asked.

"No, I said Barbados!" she reiterated.

"But isn't Barbados in Jamaica?" he asked.

"You have got to be joking, right?" she replied, visibly confused. Barbados was all Susan knew. It was her world; she could not believe that everyone did not know about this paradise made of sand, sea, and sun, which the whites used as their nature-built spa with readily available natives eager to perform for morsels of appreciation.

"Let's start over. I am David. What is your name?" he said with a cheeky smirk on his face.

"Hmm, my name is Susan," she said, while trying to contain her smile. "Where are you from?" she asked.

"I am from New Jersey," he said.

"Oh, New Jersey in Jamaica?" she said as she cried with laughter.

The look on David's face was priceless as he looked at her while shaking his head and smiling.

"Well, I hope we get to see each other again," he said as he took a leaflet out of his folder and wrote his number on it.

"Thanks, that would be nice," Susan said as she opened the conference room door and hurried off.

Susan got seated and took out the leaflet David gave her to add his number to her contacts and sent him her information via Whatsapp. As Susan still had a few minutes to spare, she decided to look through the leaflet. She was quite surprised to see a picture of David. He was the main speaker for a lecture to be held that night at seven.

"Good morning my dear, you look lovely," Mrs Knight said to Susan's surprise.

"Good morning and thank you, Mrs Knight," Susan replied as Mrs Knight took her seat right next to Susan.

As Susan quickly scanned the head table, she noticed that all of the top executives were white. She reached into her bag for her phone to turn the volume down; at the same time it vibrated. It was a message from David. As she opened the message, she saw that David had sent her an invitation to have lunch with him at a restaurant just across the street from the hotel. Susan didn't know what to make of her emotions, as she had never been asked on a date before. She was also still very cautious, as she was thousands of miles away from Velma, her anchor, in a strange land, conflicted about entertaining a stranger. Susan quickly typed that she had other plans. She was just nervous and wanted to take control of the situation, knowing that she had absolutely nothing to do that afternoon but eat alone or suffer through Mrs Knight's incessant babble.

After the seminar, which ended at five o'clock in the evening, Susan went to her room to take a short nap. She awoke soon afterwards, as she was restless and regretted that she didn't accept David's invitation. Susan decided to attend David's lecture and had less than an hour to get herself together. She hurried off to the lecture, which was being held in one of the hotel's conference rooms. At the entrance of the conference room, Susan saw a life-size poster of David—Professor David

Browne, PhD, to be exact. He was the main speaker for the event. Susan thought how David seemed really humble and never even alluded to the fact that he held a Doctorate in Philosophy and was the main speaker for the night. Susan barely was able to secure a seat since the auditorium was packed with professionals who had travelled from across the States to hear this controversial professor. It was around seven o'clock in the evening and the madam of ceremonies took the microphone to introduce David. He had a very impressive list of achievements. David stood up to a rapturous applause and took the mic. "Thank you very much for that introduction. I almost didn't know that it was me that you spoke about so eloquently, madam of ceremonies."

Susan smiled when she saw how confident and charming he was as he delivered his lecture.

"I will open tonight's lecture by asking a simple question: Life—is it a gift?" David asked as he scanned the auditorium. "I believe for some it is and for others it isn't. I know that some of you may find my response blasphemous. However, it's the only feasible, truthful answer for me.

"I have seen children die at birth; people suffer, ignored, abused and ridiculed throughout their lives, totally impoverished and left to die like animals. I have also seen the privileged ones live lavish lives without a care in this world while relishing wasteful abundance. How can anyone ignore this blatant contrast?

"Do we develop internal mechanisms to cope? For instance, saying that God has a plan, or just being thankful that we were lucky enough to escape some perilous designation? Or are we riddled with remorse and moved to philanthropy to assist the less fortunate?

"Did anyone ever stop to think how persons living in total devastation think, or if they have the luxury to think, while literally going through hell on earth? Should I be thankful that I have access to technology, properly functioning motor skills, and intact mental faculties which afford me the ability to write or speak to you now? Or should I find comfort in comparing myself to those barely living?

"Why am I made to feel guilty for even questioning? Am I questioning God? Or am I questioning man, who undoubtedly in his unquenchable greed would have contributed to this dire situation?" David paused while taking a sip of water.

The audience was silent as they took in every word that came out of his mouth. Susan was totally flabbergasted. However, nothing could have prepared Susan or the audience for what David continued to say.

Setting his glass down and clearing his throat, David asked another riveting question.

"Are all men created equal?

"To fully appreciate my view, please listen to it in its entirety. I don't believe that all men are born equal or are equal, since equal is a comparative word which means alike or identical. I do, however, believe our uniqueness transcends race, heritage, and religion. It must be embraced while recognizing and respecting the individualism of others. However, some individuals go through their entire lives not knowing their true purpose and therefore are not able to harness their potential, placing them below others whether, academically, socially, or physically.

"I have personally found resolve by simply looking at my fingerprint, how unique it is, and recognizing that I am the only one in this world with it. By doing this I am convinced that I was designed with a purpose. There is a specific task or objective that I am suitably equipped for and would masterfully accomplish better than anyone else on the planet.

"Most individuals would harshly disagree with me. No one wants to believe that they started with an unfair disadvantage, or to see themselves as not as strong, brilliant, beautiful or capable to accomplish as another. However, is this true when some persons are born with disabilities or are lost while discovering themselves? Women are physically and characteristically different from men. Blacks are genetically different from whites, so are we then debating being equal or having equal rights?

"Should we debate the issue of equality or should we embrace our individualism and strive for respect? Too often respect is introduced subliminally or subconsciously in topics related to equality. Why would we want to be equal when there is so much to garner from our myriad differences?" David concluded.

The crowd stood to their feet and gave a rapturous ovation. Susan was totally blown away. She had never in all her years heard anyone, black or white, deliver such a profound perspective on that subject matter. She also wondered if the audience, who were mainly white, just saw the speech as a demonstration of philosophical greatness or if it would stir their hearts in a tangible way with regard to the treatment of black people.

Susan wanted to get David's attention but he was surrounded by reporters, professors, and other colleagues. It was around ten o'clock at night when Susan got back to her hotel room and saw a message inviting her to dinner the following day. David seemed very pleasant and well-mannered but so did Mr Corbin, who turned out to be a ravenous beast. As she looked in the mirror, she convinced herself not to have any expectations, as they seemed to be precursors for disappointments. Susan could not stop hearing the lecture in her head that night.

The next morning as Susan made her way to the seminar, she was hoping to see David, even if it was just for a minute. There was something about his smile that was very refreshing, and she also wanted to congratulate him on his lecture the previous night. All day Susan was distracted as she kept thinking about meeting David later. The thought of cancelling again crossed her mind, which she quickly erased as the excitement of going on a date with him grew.

At the end of the seminar, Susan rushed back to the room. She wanted to look her best and hardly had time to prepare before meeting David in the lobby. She showered, tried on a million outfits, and eventually chose blue jeans which hugged her form and a pink top with a plunging neckline. She quickly stepped into her heels, sought the approval of the mirror on the wall for the final time and darted out the door.

CHAPTER EIGHTEEN

Black Lives

David's eyes lit up when Susan entered the lobby. "You look divine," he said as he stretched out his arms to hug her.

"Thank you, kind sir; you look quite smart yourself," she said with a broad smile as she embraced him. Susan had only met David the previous day but was becoming very intrigued with him the more they talked. He was funny, brilliant, and handsome.

David led the way as they headed to the restaurant across the street. As they walked they joked about the elevator incident. "Did you see her face? I thought she was going to die," said Susan.

"I am accustomed to that nonsense. It happens all of the time, but she was a bit excessive," replied David as he and Susan entered the restaurant.

"Good night," said a very pleasant hostess who greeted them and directed them to their seats. "The chef's special tonight is an Alfredo pasta with crispy mushrooms," said the hostess as she smiled at Susan, who tried to avoid full eye contact and smiled timidly back.

Susan had never been to a restaurant before and felt a bit intimidated by the names of the dishes on the menu, so she opted to make it easy on herself and ordered the special while David ordered sautéed vegetables with couscous and blackened barracuda. "Thank you," the hostess said as she took the menus and left.

"Your speech last night was very thought-provoking," said Susan.

"Thank you. I didn't expect you to attend, but I am glad you did," David said. "Those topics had been on my heart for some time. How can black men ever see themselves as equal to white men when blacks are always thrown in jail for misdemeanours? Isn't it ironic that in a country where the population is majority white, the prison population is majority black? People need to wake up and see that this high percentage of black prisoners provides goods and services, allowing businesses to benefit from cheap labour," David said, as the waiter briefly interrupted to fill their glasses with water.

Susan sat up and looked at David intently, as though in deep thought. She had never seen what David had said in that way before, but it made sense to her. Blacks were being picked off the streets, separated from their families, shipped off to prison, and their freedom restricted, all the while working for free to profit others. Here was slavery being replayed in real time right before her eyes.

"Here is your dish, ma'am, and yours, sir. Enjoy!" the waitress said as she brought the food.

"On a slightly different note, what type of music do you like?" David asked, trying to lighten the mood.

"I like calypso, reggae, and of recent, afrobeats," Susan replied.

"Calypso, what's that?" David asked.

126

"I can't believe that you have never heard of calypso, which means that you probably have never heard of Crop Over or Kadooment?" Susan said as she took a bite of her bland-tasting meal.

"I am ashamed to ask, but what is Crop Over?" David asked laughingly.

"It is a national festival in Barbados that marks the end of the cane harvesting period. It was started back in 1687, during slavery, and later revived in 1974," Susan said with a change of tone while shaking her head.

"What is wrong?" David asked.

"Nothing really, it just hit me that it started during slavery. Were the slaves rejoicing or performing for massa's pleasure, and massa celebrating because of the profits made?" Susan asked. "Also, traditionally the whites and the so-called whites start the parade, followed by the blacks, a blatant example of segregation. Anyhow, I guess you are more of a hip hop person?"

"I was when the lyrics promoted the struggle of blacks and built awareness. However, now it's just about violence, bling, and big-booty women shaking their asses in swimming pools," he said, smiling. "Also, it sickens me every time I hear black people calling each other niggas in the songs or on the streets and finding justification to support their ignorance. Isn't it just ironic that blacks are the ones promoting the use of this derogatory term and feel a sense of pride and ownership because they are allowed to use it freely while whites are forbidden to use it?" David questioned.

"With ease persons are able to change their gender at will; however, do you think the law would be so accommodating with race?" Susan asked jokingly.

"They would probably allow blacks to be identified as Indian without hassle, but never as white," David said in jest.

Susan was happy, as she had finally found a friend that she could talk to about these topics without feeling as though she was just rehashing the past.

It was getting late and Susan knew she had to get her rest since she still had to attend the seminar in the morning. "I could talk to you all night," David said as he swiped his credit card.

"I really enjoyed your company," she said as she stood to her feet.

"Have a good night and thank you for coming. Hope to see you again soon," the hostess said as she opened the door for them to exit.

As Susan stepped out the door and onto the street, she was knocked to the ground by a young man running for his life. David rushed to her assistance, helping her to her feet. She had hit her head on the pavement really hard. However, she was more shaken than injured.

The sound of sirens filled the air. The police had cornered the black man whom they were chasing when he struck her to the ground. He had nowhere to run and was visibly petrified. "Place your hands in the air slowly," bellowed this white, tattooed officer. The tension was stifling. "I said put your Goddamn hands in the air," the officer repeated. The man slowly started to raise his hands. Immediately, deafening explosions and the scent of gunpowder filled the streets. The tattooed demon in blue was firing shots relentlessly, as though he was on a range.

The first shot struck the man in his head, causing his neck to snap and parts of his brain to explode like a volcano. As the man fell to the ground, the other officers joined in and continued to perforate the unarmed, soulless black beast. "Oh my God!" Susan screamed as David tried his best to console her.

The cops still proceeded cautiously to the lifeless lump lying in the street, as though he was a threat, and kicked what was clearly his phone away from his hand. Another black man who could have been a husband, a father, a brother, was now dead. Obviously, *his black life didn't matter.*

Susan could not compose herself and cried as David pressed her face against his chest and used his shirt to dry her tears. He wanted to get her off the street and back to the hotel room. Susan was shaking and could barely support herself to walk. "Come Susan, we have to go. It's going to be okay," David said as he led her across the street back to the hotel. David knew that he could not leave Susan alone, given the state she was in. He helped her to her room, placed her on the bed, and took off her heels. The place where Susan struck her head was now swollen, so he wrapped ice in a towel and placed it on the swelling. "David, oh my God! He was unarmed," Susan cried.

"It happens all the time. We don't know what he did before, but black men are either killed or jailed for the simplest crimes, like there is a concerted effort to remove us by any means necessary," David said, while still trying to calm her. As Susan lay on the pillow, David stroked her hair and continued to dry her tears as she fell asleep. He was a total gentleman. He chose to stay with her just in case she woke up and needed anything.

In the morning, Susan arose to find David fast asleep in the chair. She had overslept and was still not in a good state to attend the seminar. She gently rubbed his shoulder to wake him. As he opened his eyes, he asked, "Are you ok?" Susan tried to be brave by nodding her head. Her eyes were swollen from all the crying she had done. David had to leave; this was his last day in New York and he was already late for his flight, but he was conflicted about leaving Susan.

"I will be okay," Susan assured him.

David gave Susan a hug and rushed out of the room while fixing his attire, nearly bumping into Mrs Knight, who was on her way to the seminar. "Sorry ma'am," he said apologetically.

"That's okay. I see you had a hard night," she said while smirking.

"Oh yes! It was!" David said innocently as they entered the elevator. He narrowly escaped her probe as he got off on the next floor.

When Mrs Knight got to the seminar, she checked her phone to see a message from Susan saying that she would not be able to attend the session. *I am sure she won't, damn little whoring black bitch. The bank paid good money for her to attend this seminar and instead she is using the opportunity to quench her crotch,* Mrs Knight said to herself, but typed 'okay, no problem.'

As Susan stayed in her room all day, she kept replaying the event. It haunted her. Black men were truly in crisis. Here was another black man taken in his prime prematurely and void of making any further contribution to his family. It seemed like all of the other races were able to build and keep their family units intact, while for blacks, the very existence of their family structure was constantly challenged.

Susan was also glad that the seminar had come to an end because she knew that she would not have been able to concentrate after what had happened. Her original plan was to use the remaining days to shop, but after the recent episode Susan was petrified and could not wait to return home. She had chosen not to tell Velma anything about the incident because she knew her mother would have been worried sick.

CHAPTER NINETEEN

Fired

That day finally came and Susan was on her way back to the rock. "Susan, I am over here!" Velma shouted when she saw her.

"Oh Mom, I missed you!" Susan said as the two ladies hugged each other and cried uncontrollably. The two talked nonstop on their way home.

As the taxi pulled in front of their house, Starboy was parked and leaning on his car. "Good evening, Susan," said Starboy. Susan almost fainted, as her father had never uttered a word to her in years.

"Good evening, sir," she said softly, while looking at her mother for support.

"How was your trip?" he asked while lifting her luggage into the house.

"It was ok, I suppose," she said, still unsure how to act. As she looked into her father's eyes she wanted to curse him but didn't out of respect.

Susan wanted to hate him but couldn't, as he was the sperm donor who contributed to her existence. Starboy took off his shoes and sat in a chair next to the door. This was one of the first times in nearly two decades that Velma, Susan, and Starboy were in the same house together. Even Velma was shocked by his actions, since after sex he never stuck around.

Starboy gestured for Susan to sit next to him. Susan's heart was racing as she reluctantly sat next to the man who had rejected her and treated her mom like shit for years. Velma also drew close, not knowing what to expect but hopeful, as she always wanted a family and nothing would please her more.

Starboy reached into his pocket and pulled out an envelope. "I heard you have a big job at the bank now and I wanted to know if you could lend me money or help me to borrow funds to pay the arrears on my car loan," Starboy asked, as he immediately ate the slap Velma served him with all her might.

"Get out of my house!" Velma roared as she sprang to her feet. Her frame was small but her spirit was not to be challenged.

Tears rolled down Velma's cheeks, not because she was weak but because she was tired of the abuse, tired of being used, and today Starboy had gone too far. Starboy moved his hand, revealing his burst lip and swollen jaw, which still had the imprint of Velma's hand. He shook his head, took up his shoes, and left, never to return. Susan had never seen her mother so angry and decided to stay as quiet as possible until she was sure her mother was calm.

The next day was work and as usual Susan arrived early. "Good morning," Susan said to Judy, the security guard.

"Good morning girl, I heard about you and your little fast self," Judy said.

"What are you talking about?" Susan asked, puzzled.

"You will soon find out," said Judy.

Susan made her way into the office, as she didn't have time to entertain Judy.

As Susan walked towards her desk, she heard giggles and whispers, and saw her colleagues pointing at her. She felt their stares on her back. This morning was like no other. This reminded her of her early childhood days at school when she struggled with her identity. However, Susan was grown now and knew who she was. She could not tell where, when, or why this new attack had originated. As she sat down in her seat determined to press forward, she tried several times to login to her system but could not get on the network. As she was about to call the IT department, she was summoned by Mrs Jackson.

As she entered the office, Mrs Knight was already seated. "Have a seat," Mrs Jackson said. "Susan, I didn't want to do this, but we are terminating your employment effective immediately," Mrs Jackson said without hesitation.

"But why? What did I do wrong?" Susan cried.

"Let's just say that your behaviour of recent is not becoming of an individual with whom we want our bank to be associated. Mr Corbin, one of our most loyal wealth customers, has expressed concerns about your lack of professionalism and inappropriate advances towards him," Mrs Jackson said while looking down at Susan.

"What?! You're kidding! This has to be a joke! That dog tried to rape me!" Susan shouted at the top of her voice.

"Oh, shut up now! What nonsense am I hearing? What would Mr. Corbin want with a woman like you?" interrupted Mrs Knight.

"A woman like me? What is that supposed to mean?" asked Susan in disbelief.

"I mean look at you. Ask yourself this question: Would he jeopardize his beautiful family for you? I think not!" Mrs Knight said sarcastically.

"Okay ladies, please let us keep this professional and not get personal," said Mrs Jackson.

"As for keeping it professional, Mrs Jackson, let's not forget that this little whoring tramp missed the seminar to have sex with a man she just met," Mrs Knight said as she pounded the desk.

Susan could not believe what she was hearing. She quickly realized that it made no sense defending her position, as the jury in the form of Mrs Knight had returned with a guilty verdict.

"If you have nothing more to say, please take your personal belongings and leave the premises. I would also advise you to be careful using the rape word, as Mr Corbin is a very influential man and it would be highly unlikely for people to take your word over his," Mrs Jackson said.

Susan dried her tears, got up and made her way to the door. She collected her personal belongings and began the innocent virgin's walk of shame, flanked by Judy, who was summoned to escort her off the property. As Susan waited for the bus she was torn. She liked her job and was fired wrongfully, her character soiled forever by a malicious rumour. Gossip just waited for a listening ear, evolving as it was passed by another weak soul eager to relish in someone else's demise.

On this small rock she called home, gossip was received like water on parched lips. People were always eager to spread vile rumours. Susan thought of all the gossip she had heard in the past. Black progressive people seemed to always be the target; rumours always circulated about how the men obtained their wealth. They were either gay, thieves, drug dealers, or a combination of all three. Women, on the other hand, were always accused of being whores and using their genitals to advance.

When blacks gossip, oh dear! Can I borrow your ear? Not just for you to hear, but for me to share this burden bestowed upon me. I have a need to sow a seed that will grow to cause the innocent, unsuspecting soul to bleed as a path of vileness proceeds. Whispers hiding in the shadows waiting to devour them with mouths filled with bloodied teeth and blackened tongues, spewing untruths, piercing the heart and soiling the virgin's bed, saying she was bred, while she lay alone in bed. Who cares if the letter "r" was the only thing inserted in this version; it would still seem more acceptable instead. The messenger bears no relevance, the truth is of no significance; however, it's all about the hurt and pain experienced that makes the difference.

Why is it so etched in us not to expect anything good from our own? Everyone seems to hate the black skin; even the blacks seem to hate it. How can we progress if we are contained in the very thing we hate? We are suspicious of it, we insult it, we try our best to dilute it, and we have lost confidence in it. Our rebirth as a people will first start by appreciating our true identity, embracing, and loving the very essence of blackness.

The seeds of discord were sown. By our actions we continue to let them bear fruit. What can we do? How can we truly address a problem when we don't identify it as a problem?

PART THREE

CHAPTER TWENTY

On The Hustle

Susan was now officially on the breadline. She wasn't about to sit idly on her ass and wait for handouts or manna to fall from the heavens. She was a go-getter just like her mother.

Before Susan was fired from her job at the bank, she was able to accumulate at least a little savings. She was not paid what she was worth but had the discipline to live within her means. Susan never tried to follow the Joneses, who for some reason always seemed to be one step ahead in spite of how hard people tried to catch up with them.

She watched her mother being exploited for years by Mr Williams, working hard day and night and only being paid enough to keep her alive to work another day. She loved the bank and learned a lot while being there, but the job was yanked from under her like a dusty rug. Job security! She thought to herself, *How can black people put their confidence in jobs where they don't make any decisions? How can they be secure when directors and managers are making decisions about them while they are sound asleep?*

Armed with these thoughts, Susan was determined to start her own business. She considered several options, but finally decided to open a restaurant. She was really excited about her idea and couldn't wait to execute it.

Over the next few days, she created her business plan and decided to approach the bank for a loan. She decided not to waste her time approaching the bank where she worked before. She knew that first her business plan would be stolen, second it would be shared, and then her loan application would be refused, in that order. Susan's scepticism about the bank wasn't fuelled by bitterness. It was developed from having intimate knowledge of how the bank operated. The bank had a social responsibility to be ethical in its operation. However, organisations are only as ethical as those who are employed within their walls.

She also saw the high interest rates that the banks charged as another mechanism to extract pounds of flesh from the weak and desperate. The banks take your money, they use it to invest and make lucrative returns for their shareholders, then charge you for poor service while making it difficult for you to withdraw your own money. The psychology behind the banking system was so amazing. How did the balance of power switch from the banks being dependent on the customers to the customers being dependent on the banks? This dynamic bore a striking similarity to slavery.

Susan decided to try the Credit Union. However, she adjusted her business plan by removing any information that would reveal her strategy to have a competitive advantage. The process was easier than the bank's process and within a couple of days she received word that the amount she applied for was approved.

Susan wished that she could have built her restaurant from the ground up on land that she owned instead of having to rent but she didn't have enough money. She found a location in a popular mall and spent the next several weeks setting up the restaurant.

The restaurant could not have come at a better time, as Velma couldn't wait to resign from her housekeeping job with Mr Clarke. She resigned for two reasons, his hypocrisy and how his behaviour changed towards her. Mr Clarke knew how impoverished Velma was and started to treat her as though he was doing her a favour, instead of their relationship being a mutually beneficial one. She was hired with the understanding that she was to clean the house, do the laundry, and cook three days a week. However, only after six months, her job description changed drastically to include grocery shopping, nursing, plumbing and carpentry. She was expected to perform all of these extra jobs for no increased pay. At the end of the day Velma would be physically and mentally drained but would have to pull herself together to prepare for the next day. It was amazing to see how this black employer started to treat his own just as massa treated the slaves for ultimate profit. Velma was treated very poorly as an employee and purposed within herself to fairly compensate her staff for their labour and not to overwork them.

It was an overwhelming task but the mother and daughter duo worked tirelessly by each other's side, supporting and encouraging each other all the way. Susan and Velma did whatever tasks they could on their own to cut costs and paid only for the labour they could afford. The ladies smiled as their hard work started to take shape. With equipment installed and utilities active, it was now time for the finishing touches.

Susan called the restaurant The Blackbelly Restaurant and Bar. The restaurant focussed mainly on local cuisine, which was evident from the menu that contained cou cou and flying fish, roast breadfruit, macaroni pie and chicken, and lamb stew from the famous blackbelly sheep.

Susan needed staff and decided to ask her family and friends for assistance. However, this proved to be a mistake, as her employees felt entitled because of their casual relationship with her and never respected Susan as their employer. In the beginning, her staff turnover was high, with hardly any staff completing the training. Blacks seemed to bend over backwards and work for next to nothing for the white man, having a sense of loyalty to him. Blacks, however, behaved very unforgivingly when they received the same or even better treatment from their black employers.

Weeks passed and Susan finally opened her doors for business. The first few months were slow but the business was still able to break even. The lines of customers started to increase with several repeat customers. This was her first business and she had a lot to learn. It was taxing, as she had to deal with some customers who at times were very rude, impatient, unreasonable, and obnoxious. There was usually no overwhelming, genuine support from black people for each other. There was a tendency to find fault and criticize every opportunity they got. The blacks supported the whites and the whites supported themselves. These customers seemed to derive pleasure from treating the serving staff badly. There wasn't a day that passed that Susan didn't hear, "I am spending my hard-earned money here, so I demand good service."

The supportive customers always wanted to give Susan and Velma advice on how to run the business. They would always say, "Black people have to support each other by buying from each other." Susan wondered how many blacks were actually able to support one another. The saying was good in theory but not practical since the money never stayed in the black man's communities.

Susan pondered that here she was renting from a white landlord, buying supplies from a white supplier, who received their supplies from a white-owned distributorship, who shipped them with a white shipping company. The problem was that black people hardly owned any top-tier businesses.

Black customers also seemed a bit more tolerant when dealing with white-owned businesses. They usually accepted the price for the product or service without debate. However, Susan's experience was the opposite.

She also had to deal with creditors who were not as lenient and had very stringent credit terms. Susan concluded that black businesses that did well should be applauded. First, it was an uphill struggle trying to obtain the finances to start the businesses and second, blacks usually didn't have collateral to invest. Black partnerships very seldom worked because of greed and a lack of trust. How could the black man truly compete with the white man, who started the race long before him?

One day as Susan was cashing, a customer asked if she would sponsor his son's rally car. The customer's son's name was Justin. Justin worked for a mechanic who would indiscriminately utilize every available square foot of land in the neighbourhood that was close to his house as his garage. Justin in his spare time would work on the car as his personal project, determined to race it someday. She wasn't a rally fan at all but this was a regular customer who had supported her from the time the restaurant opened its doors.

The restaurant at this time had been in operation for over nine months and Susan had never advertised before. She compared the sponsorship option to traditional advertising via an ad in the newspaper and as she was able to afford the amount of money Justin's dad asked for without breaking the bank, she agreed to sponsor Justin. He wanted to weld the road cage and upgrade his turbo and for that investment Susan was assured that she would have the restaurant's logo placed on the race car's bonnet. Susan signed the sponsorship agreement presented to her and made arrangements to pay the money later that day.

A few weeks passed and it was the Sunday of the rally event. Susan and Velma decided to go, as they hadn't gone out for a while. Susan also wanted to gauge for herself how impactful her advertising was. It was a bright sunny day, not a cloud in the sky. There were fans securing every possible vantage point. The whites huddled together as they capped the hills, creating an illusion of snow in the tropics. As the cars made their way onto the circuit while revving their engines, one thing was very apparent: The white drivers' cars were newer, sounded more powerful, and were sponsored by the biggest companies on the island. Finally Justin appeared. Susan's logo was the only graphic on Justin's car. As the cars roared down the track, the smell of fuel and burning tires filled the air. However, when the smoke cleared Justin had convincingly secured last place. How could he compete with cars of that calibre?

The next day Justin showed up at the restaurant to thank Susan for her support. Susan was happy to see him.

"I just want to thank you for sponsoring me yesterday," he said.

"You're welcome," Susan replied.

"I hope I didn't wreck your brand when I came last," Justin said sheepishly.

"No, you didn't. I was very proud of you because you tried your best," Susan said.

"Thanks. Thousands were there that would have seen your brand for the first time so hopefully, the exposure will bring you more business," Justin said.

"I hope it does. I could definitely do with the extra cash right now," Susan said, smiling. "By the way, did you approach any of the bigger companies for sponsorship?" she asked.

"I did, but they said that they had already used up all of the money allotted for advertising and marketing—you know how it goes," Justin replied with a shrug.

"Well, I guess blacks will just have to participate in rally for the fun of it. They have the skills but don't have the money to invest in their cars to be competitive," Susan remarked.

"Like everything else blacks find themselves lacking because of money," Justin said bitterly.

"I will continue to support you as much as I can, Justin. One of these days I promise you will have the right machine for the job," Susan reassured him.

"Thank you again. I really appreciate your kind words," said Justin as they parted ways.

Over the next few months, the business continued to do well. The restaurant was constantly improving, customer service was awesome, the facilities were clean and flawless, and the food was always tastefully prepared, with love in every dish. Susan and Velma both got their driver's licenses and bought a second-hand van for the business. The ladies also made some necessary modifications to their home. They started converting both the kitchen and the bathroom wall to wall and started to paint the entire house.

One Saturday, way before the silence of the morning was disturbed by a disgruntled Benjamin, who chose to dream about being an alarm clock instead of doing his job, Velma and Susan were already on their way to the market. Velma drove, as Susan was a horrible driver. When they got to the market, outside was still very dark but the place was a hive of activity. Several vendors with their heavy bags and boxes, with hardly any room to manoeuvre, raced against time to set up their stalls. The cool of the morning was suffocated by the heat of so many bodies rubbing against each other as customers and vendors made their way through what would seem like a maze to the untrained eye. The fragrances of Mother Nature's best filled the air with the combined scents of mud, yams, eddoes, sweet potatoes, herbs, spices, and fresh local and imported fruits. The atmosphere was overwhelming to some and excitingly intoxicating to others as the hustle began. There were faces with varied expressions. The young, the old, the dark-skinned, the light-skinned, men and women were in one place with one mind. The epicentre of black trade, disguised by dilapidated, poorly built structures, allowed those who conducted their business to innocently or craftily escape the prying scrutiny of their customers.

Velma and Susan made their way over to Eudene, their favourite vendor. Eudene was in her eighties but full of life. She didn't have a lot to offer but she was fair and her prices did not fluctuate based on her mood or the customers' profiles. She was a wise old woman, with every line in her face filled with experience, like fingertips on Braille, stories waiting to be told.

"Good morning, Mum," Velma and Susan said to Eudene as both leaned over to hug her.

"Good morning," Eudene said as the smile in her eyes lit up every pore in her face.

"How are you today?" asked Susan.

"I am great in the name of the Lord!" Eudene replied. "What can I get for you ladies today?" she asked.

This was the routine every Saturday. They would call out everything on their list like it was the first day doing business with Eudene, but the ladies loved her, and this did not faze them at all.

"We would like a pound each of marjoram, masala, turmeric, ginger and hot peppers," said Velma, who always made sure that her food was well marinated and flavourful.

"I only have a half pound of peppers." She estimated the weight without confirming with the scale. "I can throw in some extra ginger if you want, for free," said Eudene.

"No, that's quite ok," Velma said, knowing she would be ignored by Eudene.

"Thanks Mum," said Susan as she took the bags and gave Eudene the money.

As Susan leaned in to get her customary hug, Eudene pulled her closer and held her tighter than before.

"Be very careful how quickly you do things. People are envious and watching what you do when you do it, and how you do it. Not every smile means that people have your best interest at heart," whispered Eudene in Susan's ear before releasing her grip.

As they left, Susan told Velma what Eudene had said. They could find a million examples to support her statement. Susan felt disappointed, as she could never understand why black people always had to hide from each other whenever they started progressing. Why should they have to postpone expanding their house or the business, if they could afford to do it?

The restaurant was really busy and that day was hard on Velma and Susan. As if it couldn't get any worse, Velma discovered that Ronnie the porter was stealing chicken from the restaurant.

Velma became suspicious of Ronnie and later found out about Ronnie's plan from one of his workmates, who told her that Latoya and Ronnie were really good friends from school days. Ronnie had a police record, making it really hard to find a job. Velma gave him a job after hearing his story. She said everyone needed a second chance. Ronnie was really grateful and started off well. However, as time passed Latoya and her mother concocted a plan to break the restaurant down from the inside using Ronnie.

Ronnie used to place the whole, frozen chickens into the garbage to conceal them. He would then take the garbage to the dumpsters on the outside and place the bag in a car driven by Yvette. Velma actually liked Ronnie and didn't fire him because he stole. She fired him because of his associations. She would never be able to trust him again.

A year had now passed and the lease for the restaurant space was to be renewed. The landlady, Mrs Sharon, was asking for more money in rent. "Have a seat, Susan. This will not be long once you have read the document and are in agreement with it," said Mrs Sharon.

"Good morning," said Susan as she sat.

"I realise that you are doing really well from the number of customers that I see on a daily basis. I also see that you are advertising," Mrs Sharon said, rocking back in her leather chair.

"Long lines don't represent profits. You see my lines but you don't see my expenses," said Susan.

"Did you get a chance to read the lease? The increase is a mere eight hundred dollars a month. I am sure that you can handle that," said Mrs Sharon as she sipped her coffee and watched Susan intently.

"Eight hundred dollars is really excessive! That additional rental expense will not only place pressure on the business, it will definitely close it!" said Susan, who was trying her best to remain composed.

"Well, that is the figure. You either pay it or exercise your other options. I have a mall to run and there are other potential tenants lining up every day to get a space," said Mrs Sharon.

Susan ate her response as she watched the money-grubbing, pint-sized demon wrapped in white human flesh rocking back and forth. This white woman was now standing as a gatekeeper to Susan's progression. Susan signed the lease and walked out of the office.

One Saturday while Susan was walking through the food court to get to her restaurant, one of her regular customers stopped her and said, "I like supporting your business, but you need to add pudding and souse to your menu on Saturday if you want my money."

"I appreciate your business during the rest of the week, but I guess I will not get your money on Saturdays then," joked Susan.

"Well you won't get mine either, because I like my souse and my beers," said another guy.

"That's ok as well," said Susan.

150

"But why can't you just add it to the menu, seeing that so many people want it?" asked one of the men.

"Well, I don't serve it because I learnt that souse was made of the entrails and scraps left for the black slaves after massa had eaten all of the lean meat, so I could not in good conscience eat or sell it," said Susan. "Pig tongue, pig ears, pig snout—what next, pig penis and balls?!" she laughed.

"I hate to hear people talking about all this blackness, black this, black that. It makes me sick to my stomach. Always bringing up the past, like they themselves are the actual slaves who came from Africa," said one guy.

"If they love Africa so much, let them go back to Africa then! Go back to being in the jungle, swinging from tree to tree, with spears and shields and having to walk miles to hunt for food with their tribesmen and living in mud huts, without lights, or phones, or water to bathe," said another.

"The most I would do where all that shit is concerned is to dress in oversized clothing with a loud, confusing print for African week," continued the guy.

Susan could not believe the shit she had just heard and apologised to her ears for subjecting them to such auditory vileness. "Oh shut up!" she shouted. "You sound like a rambling ass!" she continued while stressing the word ass for roughly a minute. She had gotten their attention now, for sure, as you could hear a feather land. "I excuse you for being ignorant. However, I cannot excuse you for sharing your ignorance. The problem with most blacks is that we think that because we are black we know everything black and continue to convey the distortion by spreading the lies which we were taught.

"I challenge any of you here to tell me what you know about Africa. Do you know that Africa is the second-largest continent? Do you know that there are over fifty countries that make up Africa? Do you know that in terms of natural resources, Africa is the richest in the world? That is why the white man continues to this day to rob the people of what is rightfully theirs.

"Do you know any of the Kings and Queens of Africa? I can bet you know the Royal family of England, though! I can also bet you know at least three presidents of the United States of America!

"Africa, contrary to popular belief, isn't just mud huts. There are some cities in some countries in Africa where business, technology, and infrastructure would rival cities anywhere else in the world!

"If the media only highlighted depressed, poverty-stricken areas in Barbados, of which there are a few, do you think the tourists would flock to our shores?

"It is true that in some of the African countries, the level of poverty is really high, unlike anywhere else in the world. This is because the richer countries continue to exploit these African nations by raping them of their natural resources and paying them way below market value for labour and resources. It's a known strategy for these developed countries to deliberately orchestrate social unrest in these African nations, so that they can install their puppet governments and continue to exploit these countries as the world looks on.

"France, for example, still charges nearly fourteen African countries a colonization tax of nearly eighty-five percent—over five hundred billion dollars a year used to fatten white French men while the black African continues to wither away! How can the world continue to watch this injustice? These African countries then have to borrow back their own money and pay high-interest rates. This is totally absurd! However, African leaders fear for their lives as all of those leaders who have tried to become totally independent from the claws of France were killed," Susan said as tears filled her eyes. The discourse weighed heavily on Susan that day, along with her other challenges, causing her to be depressed the entire day.

The ladies had to make some tough decisions. They had to halt renovations on the house, some of the staff's hours had to be reduced, and one person was made redundant. The business advertising was suspended and the menu had to be shortened. All of these changes had an adverse effect on the business.

Over time the numbers decreased and Susan and Velma were struggling daily to keep the doors open. They had to use the day's sales to buy stock for the next day and beg the staff to work some weeks without being paid in order to accumulate enough money to pay the additional rent. The creditors became impatient and only accepted full cash payment on delivery of the stock. Some days the natural gas would be turned off while they were preparing the meals. The credit union loans officer started calling relentlessly. Their credit rating took a nosedive, impacting their ability to borrow money from other financial institutions. The bills were coming in rapidly.

One day as they were driving, the van ran out of gas on the highway. It was inevitable that it would stop at some point, as there were only so many miles one could drive on an empty tank. The van also wasn't insured, so it was in their best interest for the vehicle to break down when it did. Susan and Velma couldn't afford to service or buy parts for the van. They decided to call the bailiff, who they were avoiding for a while, to collect the van. The vehicle was towed from the side of the road and they were notified that a bill for the wrecker service would be sent in the mail.

Velma and Susan were fighting tooth and nail not to give up the restaurant but it was only a matter of time before they started to fall behind on the rent. The restaurant was the only source of income for Velma and Susan, and the bills at home also started to pile up. Velma was a hustler and would collect bottles if she had to in order to survive. However, after being the co-owner of the restaurant she didn't feel inclined to return to that hustle. Velma wondered if it was pride. It seemed like the higher one rises, the higher their lowest bar also becomes.

As Velma pondered, an idea struck her. She thought about selling food from their house. She told Susan about it and Susan wasn't that keen at first, but they literally had no options. They had to think quickly, as they were now two months behind on their rent.

"I think that we should remove the equipment that we need to continue the business at home from the restaurant as soon as possible, before the equipment is seized for non-payment," said Susan.

"But how will we do that without raising an alarm?" asked Velma.

"We will arrange to do a thorough cleaning on Sunday when the restaurant is closed. We will make sure that the freight truck is there on location to transport the equipment from the mall to our house," said Susan.

"What about the staff?" asked Velma.

"Well, we will definitely have to tell them. I wouldn't want them turning up for work to find closed doors," said Susan.

Saturday came and Velma and Susan struggled with the business as usual. Business was awful, as their customer base was relatively nonexistent now.

One of their customers, who realised that the standards and customer base of the business had dropped significantly, called Susan aside and said, "Maybe you should consider placing a white person as the face of your business."

Susan was totally repulsed by the suggestion. "I would prefer to shrivel up in a corner and die before I did that," she said while making a spitting gesture. "That goes against everything I stand for and believe in and it is this mindset that continues to worsen the black man's plight," she continued.

At the end of the business day Susan called the three staff together to inform them that they would be closing the business and starting operations from her home. Susan made sure she paid them from the day's takings before they left for the evening.

Sunday came and Susan and Velma arranged with the freighter to meet them at the mall at eight o'clock. When they got there, they saw that the doors were padlocked and a notice saying the premises were closed until further notice was stuck on the door.

Susan was devastated and kept banging on the door. "This can't be right!" said Susan in frustration.

"This is just unfair. What are we supposed to do now, Mom?" asked Susan. "When will this shit stop, Mom? It has to stop! Mrs Sharon isn't a successful business woman because she is better or brighter than you or I," cried Susan. "She is where she is because her forefathers exploited our forefathers and left a golden spoon for her. Now she is using that blasted spoon to take food off our plates," continued Susan.

Susan was having a meltdown. Velma stood there and for the first time felt powerless. She was just as frustrated as Susan but didn't want to vent, fearing it would only make the problem worse. The tense air was interrupted by the ringing of Susan's phone. It was David; Susan would have ignored the call if it was anyone else.

She really liked talking to David. He was one of the few people besides Velma who comforted her when she was in a sad place. Over the years Susan and David had kept in contact, messaging each other regularly and becoming really good friends.

"Hi Susan, how are you doing?" asked David.

"I am fine," Susan replied, while trying to hold back tears.

"Why are you crying, Susan? What happened?"

"Remember I told you about the landlady raising the rent?"

"Yeah, you did," David replied.

"Well, things got worse," Susan explained. "We couldn't afford the rent and had to close the business," she cried.

"Oh no, I am so sorry to hear," said David.

"They have also seized all of our equipment, which we still have to pay for," said Susan

"Is that even legal?" David asked.

"I don't even know, David. These white people just get to do whatever they want," said Susan.

"So what are you going to do now?" David asked.

"Well, we wanted to start up the business at home but it's not the most ideal situation," Susan said.

"I understand. Is there anything that I can do to help?" asked David.

There was no answer on the other line.

"Hello! Susan! Hello!"

Susan's battery had died. Susan was really upset with herself that she didn't charge her phone properly.

David's vacation was coming up in a few weeks and he decided to spend it in Barbados. He was really concerned about Susan and wanted to see her again. He also wanted to experience for himself this beautiful island Susan called home. He had planned to surprise Susan when he got to the island. David was convinced now more than ever to book his ticket and spend his vacation in Barbados.

CHAPTER TWENTY-ONE

A New Start

A week passed and Velma and Susan were still determined to start a business from home on their small three-burner stove. They started by cooking all the food they had access to. Persons who knew about Velma's cooking continued to support her. However, the location was not central or high traffic. The few meals that they sold were barely able to pay their bills. They didn't have a cent more to do anything else. Their kitchen was small and congested. It was not adequate for cooking volume. They didn't have any stainless steel counters. There was no commercial stove and equipment, or any room for expansion. Even if they wanted to expand or serve more customers, they couldn't.

Hardly anyone in the neighbourhood bought food from Susan and Velma, especially since the village rum shop started providing hot meals to compete with them. The daily takings were really meagre. Susan remembered the days when they were in the mall and she had to deposit funds twice daily for the Blackbelly Restaurant and Bar so as not to have so much money in her possession. Now she could hold all of the money from her sales in a clenched fist. It was hardly anything to conceal.

No one said anything to their faces, but it seemed like the entire village was happy at their misfortune. It wasn't personal. It just seemed like something black people did. People, for no apparent reason, would be jealous of your achievements. Instead of being motivated by you and raising their bar, they preferred that your bar be lowered so that they wouldn't feel like failures.

It was Saturday night and the ladies didn't have to hustle in the morning to go to work or go to church or do anything. Susan and Velma stayed up talking all night about everything under the sun. The two ladies passed out on the chairs without bathing or brushing their teeth as they were accustomed. This was a true testament to how tired they both were.

The rain had just started to fall as Susan looked through her window. She watched as a frail old lady, wearing an oversized, beautiful blue dress and a white hat with black shoes and a black handbag walked by. The old lady had a cane and was placing all of her weight on it for support as she slowly dragged her feet along, making the routine trip to church. Susan watched as cars passed by, none of them stopping to give the old lady a ride although some of them were going to the same church.

Is this Christ, the answer? Is this the abundant life the holy book speaks of? Where neighbours blatantly ignore each other's needs, believing that church started from the inside the building? As Susan continued to watch she thought about how spirituality was during and before slavery. How did her forefathers praise, worship, and serve their creator? How did their relationship with their creator influence their actions toward each other? Susan desired to know the truth since church as she knew it seemed hypocritical and false.

She remembered times when she had attended church where the members would be the holiest of holy on Sundays as they entered the church and exited as demons as soon as the service was over. The church's focus seemed to have shifted from loving your brother to loving your brother's money. Some congregants were gently persuaded to give with a cheerful heart every Sunday, while the band masterfully played in the background. On the other hand, for other congregation members, scare tactics such as the hellfire message worked to release their tithes and offerings.

The message of salvation seemed to be directly linked to increased membership, which increased profits. What amazed Susan was how easily these church members would ignore their brothers who were on the street begging for bread in their quest to give to Jesus Christ.

It was now Monday afternoon and outside was hot and sunny. Velma chose to take the opportunity to wash her clothes, as she hadn't washed them for a while. As she sat on a bucket in the backyard, reaching into the tub, she heard someone calling.

"Good afternoon, Susan! Good afternoon!"

Velma got up and made her way to the front of the house, where she saw a tall, dark and extremely handsome guy. He was well-dressed in his blue jeans and white V-neck T-shirt and all white sneakers.

"Hi, can I help you?" said Velma as she approached him.

"I guess you are Velma, right? Susan's mom?" the guy said with his American accent.

"Oh Lord, David!" exclaimed Velma. "You must be David!"

"Yes, I am. Sorry for my manners earlier; I should have said Miss Lynch," replied David.

"You are just as Susan described. She told me so much about you," Velma said excitedly, revealing Susan's crush. "Did she know that you were coming?" asked Velma.

"No, she didn't. I wanted to surprise her," replied David.

"Come, let's get you out of this sun before you bake. She should soon be home." Velma motioned him inside.

No sooner did they get into the house than they heard Susan's voice in the distance.

"Hide behind this door," Velma told David.

As David hid behind the bedroom door, keys could be heard rustling as Susan tried to find the right key for the door. David's heart was beating so loudly that he thought his hiding place would be compromised. Finally, Susan was inside the house. "Good afternoon, Mom."

"Good afternoon," Velma replied while smiling from ear to ear.

"Why are you smiling like a Cheshire cat?" asked Susan.

"Well, I have a surprise for you, dearest," said Velma. "Come on out!"

David could not deal with the suspense any longer, knowing that Susan was in the same house, so he slowly opened the door, revealing himself.

"Mom! Look out, there is someone behind you!" Susan screamed as she nearly yanked Velma's arm out of the socket to get her away.

Susan went through a range of emotions, from fear to shock to excitement. It was just too much for her brain to process at once so Susan fainted and fell to the floor. "Susan!" Velma and David yelled together as though rehearsed.

As they both rushed to Susan's assistance she opened her eyes.

"David?! Is that really you, David?" Susan said while trying to catch her breath.

"Yes, it is!" he replied as he held out his arm to help her up. Susan for the first time lost all of her inhibitions and leapt into David's arms, wrapping her legs around him as he struggled to keep his balance. She then held his face with both her hands and kissed him passionately. Susan by no stretch of her imagination expected to see David, but she was overjoyed and could not contain her emotions.

The two had so much to catch up on. They talked while Velma prepared her famous macaroni pie and baked chicken, filling the house with mouth-watering aromas. Velma served lunch on the small wooden table, which had to be propped with a book to stop it from rocking. There were only two chairs, both with torn, tacky upholstery. Velma opted to sit on the sofa and ate the burnt ends of food directly from the pot. Susan was concerned about how David would feel in her very humble home. However, David seemed very comfortable and not at all bothered. He was just happy to be in Susan's company. The two talked and laughed for hours as Velma watched.

"Was it difficult finding our house, David?" Velma asked.

"No actually, there were a lot of taxis and when my taxi came, I just gave the driver your address and he knew the area. When we reached the neighbourhood, the driver asked some guys if they knew Susan," continued David.

"They can afford to do that here. Barbados is so small and everybody knows everybody," Velma said, smiling.

"There were a lot of taxi drivers at the airport, though, and even one big tour bus which a lot of tourists were boarding. How are these taxi drivers able to provide for their families if the competition is so stiff?" asked David.

"And on the flip side they only issue a few tour bus permits," said Susan.

Susan saw David staring pensively at the ceiling and decided to lighten the mood.

"Mom, I have a bit of trivia for you. Who, or what, am I? I am a very wealthy white businessman. I own a tour company. We are able to promote ourselves by going places to reach the tourists before they reach Barbados, enticing them with our sunny tours to tan their weathered heads. Who, or what, am I? "Susan said with a smirk.

"I know who that is! You are wicked, Susan," Velma laughed.

"I have another one, Mom! I am a construction magnate who chose to move the earth and do as I pleased. I own half of the island's land. I once told a story of starting from humble beginnings which you would have to be a cow to believe. My brother is also busy and owns half of the island's businesses. Who, or what, am I?" Susan asked as both she and her mom laughed hysterically.

Susan continued, "I pretend to be a white businessman. I have one of the largest contracts for providing housing, while the average black contractor can't get a contract to build a shed. If you believe this is by coincidence, mark my words, it isn't. Your head would have to be rock hard like cement to believe so. Who, or what, am I?"

"I have one!" Velma said. "I am a white man, not a fat man but a stout man. I own over four hundred rental cars while black people struggle to get even one rental permit. Who, or what, am I?" asked Velma as both of them chuckled.

David looked bewildered, as he could not figure out the answers to any of the trivia questions. Plus the ladies were laughing heartily, as though it was a private joke.

"I don't get it," said David.

"You wouldn't! You would have to be a Barbadian to understand, but I will tell you later," Susan said assuredly as she squeezed his hand. "Simply put, there are some things that white people with money can afford that you definitely can't afford without."

CHAPTER TWENTY-TWO

A Thief In The Night

As customers continued to spread the word about Velma's cooking, the numbers started to increase. The takings were not significant but made Velma and Susan hopeful. One humid night, the wind was still, and both ladies had retired early, as the house was very hot.

A man dressed in all black from head to toe—in a black hoodie, black skinny jeans, and black shoes, with a black scarf tied around his mouth to conceal his features—placed his hand through a broken shutter and quietly opened the latch. As he was walking past Susan's room, she lay there fast asleep in only her underwear. He paused for a minute to watch Susan's curvaceous body lying on the bed. Her legs were opened wide from east to west and her exposed, perky breasts were inviting. This thief in the night was on a mission to steal money and valuables, but after seeing Susan's body he would have easily aborted his plan in order to nurse on her nipples.

He had watched Susan for years, imagining her in the most provocative positions. Now here she was in the flesh, in all her glory. He was conflicted as the means to quench his lust was within arm's reach, but he had a drug addiction which required money. The intruder continued on as quietly as possible, being careful not to knock over anything. He stealthily headed towards a black bookshelf situated in the corner of the living room and started rummaging through the books and items on it, looking for money and valuables. At the same time, Velma got up to pee. As she stepped out of her room into the living area, she heard the rustling sounds. Still groggy, she didn't register the intruder at first. However, as she focussed, she saw a beam from the intruder's torch light. Velma's heart raced and in that split second she was faced with a choice dilemma. There were six million ways for this son of a bitch to die. She had to choose one. At this time Velma's brain placed the request from her bladder on temporary hold as it chose to process more pertinent matters.

Velma tiptoed to the kitchen, less than five steps away, and quietly took up the sharpest knife she could find. Velma could hear her own heart knocking frantically at her brain's door. She then walked cautiously back to the living room with the knife in hand to find that the intruder was not there. She was now sweating profusely and felt uneasy, as she didn't know where he was. Fear took over and her bladder, realising that there was a delay in sending messages to her brain, broke protocol and emptied its contents.

Velma glanced at the bookshelf and could see that the golden bracelet her granny had given her was missing. At this point she didn't know if the intruder had left or not and decided to check on Susan. To Velma's relief Susan was still sleeping peacefully. Velma walked over to Susan to wake her up. However, she froze in her tracks when she realized that what she thought was a shadow was actually the intruder, who didn't notice Velma, as he was facing the window and trying to take off his pants.

Velma screamed at the top of her lungs while flying through the air with the knife pointed. Velma was ready to drive her dagger into the heart of this bloodsucking vampire who had no regard for her privacy. The guy narrowly escaped the blade slitting his throat as he scrambled to quickly regain his composure. He was horny only a moment ago but now he was in a battle for his life.

Susan jumped up, screaming and confused, but seeing her mother in danger she sprang into action as quickly as possible. She picked up an iron which was resting on the ground and flung it with all her might, striking the assailant.

Velma continued her attack, kicking and jabbing. She tried her best to rid her household of this threat, and her aim was to protect Susan and herself at all cost.

Susan, seeing that her mother had gotten hold of the thief's shirt, took up one of her heels and clobbered him in the back of his head. The thief, realising that he picked the wrong house to rob, shook off the blow that Susan delivered and returned one of his own, knocking Susan to the ground. Velma was scratching, tugging, and screaming erratically. The houses in the neighbourhood lit up one by one. The dogs started to howl and bark. Even Benjamin got in on the action as he curiously strutted around the premises, evidently upset about the ruckus inside which was disturbing his rest.

Velma was relentless and by this time had snatched the scarf off the thief's face. The guy, realising he had nowhere to run and his identity was revealed, pulled a Glock from his waist. He pointed it at Velma. Susan was back on her feet by this time and jumped between the gunman and her mother as she shouted, "Jaden, no!"

It was too late; Jaden had pulled the trigger. The bullet ripped a hole in the side of Susan's head. The explosion lit up the house and the blast rocked the neighbourhood. Blood was everywhere. The smell of gunpowder and scorched flesh and hair filled the house.

Susan had tried to save her mother, heroically taking a bullet for her. Now, Susan lay prostrate on the ground in a pool of blood, blinking as if to say goodbye. Velma screamed and rushed to Susan's aid, giving no regard to the fact that the armed thief was still there. He simply reached for his bag and stepped over Susan's body as he left the room.

Susan's life was fading quickly. "Oh God! No! Don't take my daughter! Take me instead! Please God, be merciful!" Velma cried.

Screams filled the air as the news quickly spread. Sirens wailed as the blue and red lights, along with the paramedics, took centre stage. The paramedics, though professional, looked really distressed as they carried out their duties while the police rudely tried to get information. Velma could not contain herself. She cried a mother's cry for her daughter. She begged God to spare Susan's life as death was knocking at Susan's door.

The paramedics rushed Susan to the hospital as Velma sat beside her, crying uncontrollably and periodically wiping her tears on her shirt, still stained with the blood of her daughter.

The ambulance arrived and the surgeons wasted no time prepping Susan for surgery as they rushed her to the operating theatre. Velma waited for seven long hours as well-wishers, not knowing what to say, held their heads down, hiding their solemn expressions.

Finally, the head surgeon entered the lobby. "Miss Lynch, I am Dr. Greaves," said the doctor.

"How is she, Doc? Is she going to make it?" cried Velma.

The doctor paused. Velma screamed, "Oh no! God, no! Not my baby!"

Doctor Greaves, on realizing that his pause gave Velma the wrong impression, quickly tried to console her. "Miss Lynch, Susan is still alive. I am sorry for pausing. I was just thinking of what a fighter your daughter is. She is in a coma but she wants to live."

Velma finally pulled herself together and called David, who had already heard and was on his way to the hospital. When David got to the hospital, the two hugged as Velma started to cry again. They spent the entire day at the hospital, waiting for any new information from the doctors. The next day, David offered to help Velma clean up the mess from the ordeal, as he knew that it would have been hard for her to do it alone. As they were cleaning, they heard a knock at the door. It was the police. Velma opened the door and was greeted by a remarkably pleasant officer, unlike some of his obnoxious colleagues who masked their insecurities behind their uniform. He had come to tell her that they had caught Jaden and charged him with unlawful breaking and entering, aggravated assault, and attempted murder. Velma was relieved upon hearing that Jaden was in police custody, as she had felt unsafe with him still on the run.

Velma connected even more to David through the traumatic experience and loved him dearly like the son she never had. David extended his stay and for the next couple of weeks, the two took turns staying by Susan's bedside, hoping that someday she would finally open her eyes.

CHAPTER TWENTY-THREE

The Dream

It was a Wednesday and Velma rose early on her own accord, as the morning wasn't announced by Benjamin as usual. Benjamin had apparently gotten himself into trouble when he followed a yard fowl in Maisey's backyard. There had been sounds of chains pulling, dogs barking, snarling and gnashing of teeth. Witnesses testified that they saw a feathered halo floating above Maisey's paling. Old Benjamin was never seen or heard after that. The thirsty old cock would be missed.

Velma got to the hospital and saw David asleep in the chair, as he had stayed by Susan's side all night. Susan's room was filled with get well cards, flowers, and balloons from friends, family, and foes. Even Mrs Knight organized for all of the employees at the bank where Susan previously worked to buy a get well soon banner and chose to deliver it herself. As soon as Mrs Knight entered the room David woke up.

"You look vaguely familiar. I am trying to put a name to your face," said Mrs Knight.

"Oh, I don't think we were formally introduced but we ran into each other at the hotel in New York a few months back when I was rushing to catch my flight," David said.

"Yes, I remember you now. You rushed out of Susan's room early that morning, fixing yourself," Mrs Knight said while glancing at Velma. "You seem like a decent gentleman but Susan should have been more responsible, as her reckless behaviour caused her to lose her job," Mrs Knight continued.

"Reckless behaviour? What are you insinuating?" David asked as he slightly raised his voice.

"Insinuating? There was nothing to insinuate. It was quite clear that what had happened the night before caused her to call and say that she would not be able to attend the last day of the seminar," said Mrs Knight as she squared her shoulders.

"Susan witnessed a man being shot by the police the night before and was really distraught. I spent the night trying to console her," David said, trying his best to remain civil and respectful.

Velma was confused, as she was hearing all of this for the first time. She was, however, able to piece the puzzle together. "So it was you who got my daughter fired?" Velma said as she looked around the room, as though searching for a loose object to clobber Mrs Knight.

"Please let cool heads prevail, as this is not the time or place to discuss issues like this, given Susan's condition," Mrs Knight said as she placed the banner on a chair and hurriedly left the room.

Velma was fuming and attempted to follow her but was quickly restrained by David.

As Susan slept, a towering figure of a man appeared at the doorway. She could not make out his features but his silhouette slowly transformed into majestic blackness. His skin was hardened with torturous scars but it glistened like gold and his eyes pierced her very core.

"Do not be troubled, my child, for I am the spirit of your forefather Amare," he said as he stretched out his hand to hold hers. As she placed her hand in his, she noticed how her hand became like a baby's, not just in size but in texture. Instantly, her eyes were opened and her senses were renewed. His hand was hot and felt as though water was running through it. He never uttered another word as he guided her through the open doorway.

As she stepped outside she saw black men and women of all shades and sizes, some naked and some well-dressed, representing all of the socio-economic classes. This sea of black people which she saw had massive chains around their necks and their feet. They were organized into tiers, with those at the higher levels also holding the ones below them with smaller chains. As Susan looked up she saw seven white giants who were holding all of the chains. Some chains were longer than others, some were invisible, and some even appeared to have been broken before and repaired.

Susan wept as she watched and realized that in spite of the black man's position, there were no black giants, as he was still totally dependent on how much was given by the white giants. As the tears streamed down her face, she felt her tiny hands being squeezed gently, as if to reassure her that everything would be ok.

Susan held on even tighter as she felt her body being lifted from the ground. Almost immediately, she was hovering high in the air, where she could see endless land. Faceless black souls were being consumed by the earth like seeds being planted as they worked. As they disappeared beneath the soil, gold sprang to the surface, which other blindfolded black souls took to the white giants.

These black souls seemed all too content to tighten each other's blindfolds and resisted any attempt to remove them. They were fed day and night by the giants and depended on them for everything, whether directly or indirectly.

As Susan looked farther in the distance, she saw black men and black women dressed in suits sitting behind desks secured in place by thick ankle-deep mud in the open field. Their faces were hardened and their smiles lacked passion, as their vessels did not contain hearts. They were purpose-driven and focussed, moving around liberally. However, as Susan looked closely, she saw the invisible chains around their necks and feet.

There was also a giant standing by a bell tower that reached to the sky. As the giant rang the bell, the land vibrated with deafening clanging. Suddenly everyone stopped what they were doing and headed toward the sound as though in a trance. A massive portrait of a big, black giant with high cheekbones, a broad nose, thick lips and woolly hair, wearing a crown made of thorns, was presented to all who gathered. The crowd erupted into a mad frenzy, gnawing and clawing at the image until they shredded it into indistinguishable pieces.

Susan was then led behind the bell tower, where she saw massive black tombstones at the heads of black graves. All of the tombstones were different in shapes and sizes, each with unique inscriptions: black talent, black father, black son, black hero, black brilliance - the graves stretched for miles. Susan saw that these graves were filled to capacity but still continued to accept young black hearts, beating hearts, hearts still full of life, hearts that were being violently forced into these graves by their own kind. Oh, how rivers flowed from swollen eyes as vultures blackened the blue skies and lost black babies walked aimlessly towards the horizon with their empty hands outstretched to those who passed by.

Susan felt as though she was losing her grip and started to panic as she was still high in the air. She tried really hard not to let go as she dug her nails bone deep into flesh. "Susan, Susan!" Velma exclaimed.

Susan slowly opened her eyes and realized that it was her mother's hand. As Susan's focus became clearer she smiled from her heart when she saw Velma and David. Susan could hear and see but still didn't have much control of her motor functions as she lay on the bed, drifting in and out of sleep. Velma saw a sparkle in Susan's eyes amidst all of the tubes, the machinery and monitors, and felt comforted in her spirit that Susan would have a full recovery.

Velma started to cry as she watched Susan lying on the bed. She cried because she was happy and sad at the same time. She was happy because Susan was still alive and sad because she nearly lost the love of her life. Susan watched her mother as she fought back the tears. She wanted to talk to her but she couldn't. Susan's near brush with death made her think about her life and her purpose here on earth.

She was too perfectly designed for it to be a coincidence. Her habitat was too masterfully engineered for her to survive and enjoy for it to be by chance. The air she breathed, the water, the plants, the sea, the sun, the minerals—trying to list the countless splendours would be a futile endeavour. The sheer magnificence of creation humbled her when she thought of being one of billions, present and past, on a planet that was only one of millions in an incomprehensible universe.

Susan felt insignificant and special at the same time to be a part of this grand plan. This grand plan could never have been created for whites to lord over blacks but for all men to live as one. As time passed, the dream never left Susan. The dream had awakened her consciousness. She was now determined not only to break the chains but to become a giant herself and pave the way for other black giants.

Continue processing...

Made in the USA
Middletown, DE
16 March 2021

35642216R00102